GERTRUDE,
GUMSHOE

D0064172

ROBIN MERRILL

New Creation Publishing

Other Books by Robin Merrill

FICTION

Shelter

Daniel

Grace Space: A Direct Sales Tale

The Witches of Commack, Maine

DEVOTIONALS

The Jesus Diet: How the Holy Spirit Coached Me to a 50-Pound Weight Loss

More Jesus Diet: More of God, Less of Me, Literally

New Creation Publishing
Madison, Maine

This is a work of fiction. Names, characters, businesses, organizations, places, events, and incidents are either the products of the author's imagination or used in a fictitious manner. Any resemblance to actual persons, living or dead, or actual events is purely coincidental.

Cover by Taste & See Design
Formatting by PerryElisabethDesign.com

ISBN-13: 978-0692689097
ISBN-10: 0692689095

Library of Congress Control Number: 2016911223

For all the friends who love Gertrude as much as I do

1

No matter how many times she counted her cats, Gertrude still kept coming up one short. But she wasn't quite sure *which* kitty was missing exactly. It's hard to count cats in an over-stuffed mobile home, especially when they won't hold still.

After several failed attempts, Gertrude realized that all she had to do was write down the cats' names as she spotted them. She grabbed some scrap paper out of one of her scrap paper bins. First on the roll call was Sunshine, who was napping atop a pile of linens, which were on top of a box of lightbulbs, which was on top of two twin size mattresses leaning against the wall. Next was Rain. Gertrude caught him strolling down one of the narrow paths carved out between stacks of her belongings and knelt to give him a soothing neck scratch. She wrote his name down, and then grunted as she stood up to head toward the bedroom, which was where Blizzard liked to hang out.

In this manner, eventually, Gertrude deduced that Tornado was the missing cat.

She wove all over her trailer calling his name. But there was no Tornado. "He must've gotten out somehow," she said to Hail, who seemed to agree. At least, he didn't argue. So Gertrude put on a sweatshirt—it was September, so not quite jacket weather in Maine yet—and then she and her walker headed out into the trailer park.

Gertrude lived in trailer number three. Her park consisted of twelve trailers, located on either side of a narrow drive. Each end of the one-way road spilled out onto Route 150 in the small town of Mattawooptock.

Gertrude started at the trailer to her right. She knew its residents weren't home right now, which was good, as she wasn't really in the mood for human contact. She bent over and looked under the trailer as she called Tornado's name. Then she walked around the trailer, looking for any signs of a wayward feline. She found none, so she moved on to the next trailer. She knew that Old Man Crow—that's what the neighborhood kids called him—was home. He was always home, and she could hear his television. She thought about knocking on the door and actually asking him if he'd seen Tornado, but he was an ornery old coot, and she didn't want to deal with it. Old Man Crow was all fancy and had skirt panels around the bottom of his trailer, so Gertrude couldn't see underneath. He also had curtains, so she couldn't see inside. She moved on.

She reasoned that the next trailer would be empty too. Its new residents had moved in a few months ago. Gertrude had seen a woman and two kids and had assumed the woman was a single mother. She looked under the trailer and called to Tornado. Then she took a stroll around trailer number nine, alternately calling and listening. As she came around to the front again, she thought she heard a meow. She froze and held her breath. There it was again. She bent over and looked under the trailer again. Nothing. She stood. And waited. And there it was. The cry for help was muffled, but she knew that voice anywhere. It was Tornado. And it sounded like he was *inside* the trailer.

Gertrude took three steps closer to the door. "Tornado?"

Nothing.

She took another step closer. "Tornado?"

She waited. Still nothing.

She climbed the steps and stood in front of the door, leaning forward so her face was only inches from the door. "Tornado? Are you in there?" She heard a squeak, and a burst of adrenaline shot through her. She pounded on the door. "Hello? Hello? Is anyone home?" Nothing. She pounded again. Nothing. She looked around the trailer park to see if anyone was watching her. She saw no one. She reached for the doorknob. It was locked. *What on earth?* Gertrude thought. *No one locks their house in Mattawooptock.* She put her lips as close to the door as they could get without actually touching the door and yelled, "Don't worry, Tornado! I will get you out! I'm going to call the fire department again!" As Gertrude stood waiting for the cat to answer her, the door opened, and Gertrude found herself eye to eye with a little boy. A little boy who was holding her cat.

"Please don't, ma'am," the boy said.

"Don't call me ma'am. I'm not old. That's my cat."

"OK."

"So give him to me." Gertrude reached out with both hands, and the boy shrank back in fear, taking the cat with him. Gertrude pushed the door open and stepped into the dark trailer. "That's my cat."

"OK."

As Gertrude's eyes adjusted to the dimness, she saw a young girl sitting cross-legged on the floor in front of a game of Uno. Gertrude's eyes flitted around the room. It was neat as a pin. "Why aren't you in school?"

The little boy started to cry.

"Why are you crying?"

He didn't answer.

Gertrude looked at the girl. "Why is he crying?"

"You're scaring him," the girl said.

"Why? I'm not scary."

The girl hesitated. Then, "You kind of are," she said.

Gertrude sighed. "Look, I'm not mean. I just want my cat."

The boy nodded, sniffed, and then held Tornado out with two ramrod-straight arms. He did not move closer to Gertrude. Tornado dangled helplessly from his little hands. Gertrude grabbed him and brought him into her ample bosom. Tornado rubbed his head on her chin and began to purr.

"Why do you have my cat?"

"Sorry," the girl said. "He was on our steps. We didn't know he was yours."

"OK," Gertrude said. "No harm done then." She stood there for a few seconds, unsure of what to do. She wanted to go, but she knew something was wrong. "So, what's going on here? Why aren't you two in school?"

The boy started crying again.

"Stop crying!" Gertrude snapped. "I'm not even being scary anymore!"

"He's scared because we're all alone. Come here, Carl," she said, and patted the floor beside her. Carl went and sat.

He looked so forlorn, Gertrude thought about giving him the cat back, but then decided against it. "What do you mean you're all alone?" she asked.

The two kids exchanged a look.

"Oh, just tell me," Gertrude snapped.

"Do you have any grandkids?" the girl asked.

"Grandkids?!" Gertrude cackled. "I'm not old enough for grandkids! Stop changing the subject. Where is your mother?"

The girl took a deep breath. "She hasn't come home yet. She works nights. She leaves us here alone when she goes to work because she can't afford a babysitter, but it's OK because I'm eight and I watch my little brother. He's five," she explained.

"OK, where does she work?"

"We don't know. She got a new job. I'm not sure where it is, but she is always home when we get up. And she takes us to school. But when we're home alone, we're supposed to lock the door and not answer it, because she'll get in trouble if the cops find out we're home alone."

"Uh-huh," Gertrude said. She couldn't put her finger on it, but something about this story just wasn't sitting right with her. "Well," she said, looking around, "I'm here now, so let's turn some lights on."

Gertrude flipped the kitchen light switch and set Tornado down on the counter. He instantly jumped off.

Gertrude walked around the bar and into the small kitchen. She picked up a pile of papers from the countertop and began to sift through them. "What's your name?" she asked the girl without looking up.

"Sophia."

"OK, Sophia, can you think of anywhere that your mother might be?"

"No."

"Well, how about your dad?" Gertrude looked up. "Should I call him?"

"No." Sophia's lower lip trembled. "He didn't want us anymore. That's why our mother took us."

"Hmm. OK." Gertrude stuck several expired coupons into her pocket and then saw something helpful. A pay stub. From Private Eyes.

Private Eyes was a strip club in downtown Mattawooptock. Gertrude had never been there and had never heard anything good about the place. It seemed this was where the kids' mother was working nights, and not for very much money apparently. The paystub was for 159 dollars. *There's a good chance she makes more than that in tips,* Gertrude thought, and then felt guilty for having such a thought in front of the children.

"Tell you what," she said, coming back around the bar toward the kids. Both kids stared at the walker. "I'll go down to where she works and ask around."

Sophia's eyes lit up. "Really? Can we come?"

"No," Gertrude said quickly. "Do you have any pictures of her?" She began to stroll around the trailer, looking for photos.

"I don't think so," Sophia said.

"You have *zero* pictures of your mother? How is that possible?"

Sophia shrugged.

"OK, well, what's her name?"

"Lori."

13

"OK. If you'll let me use your phone, I'll try to go find Lori. I just need to call the CAP bus."

The CAP bus was actually a van, driven by volunteers. CAP stood for Community Action Program. People in need or those with disabilities could call the CAP bus, and it would take them to necessary destinations such as medical appointments, job interviews, and worship services. She wasn't sure how she was going to get them to take her to the strip club, but she was going to try.

2

When the van pulled into the trailer park, Gertrude was back by her own steps waiting. She had left Tornado with the kids. They had seemed to need him more than she did at the moment.

When the van stopped, Gertrude was relieved to see that Norman was driving. Norman was a retired bus driver who volunteered to drive the CAP bus several days a week. Gertrude thought he was kind of hot, with his shaggy hair and tattoos, though he was *much* too old for her.

"Norman!" she exclaimed as she climbed into the middle seat of the van. "All alone today?"

"So far, yep. I had to take a few guys to the drugstore, but since then, things have been slow."

"Well, good, 'cause I don't want any witnesses for this."

Norman looked at her in the rearview mirror and there might have been fear in his eyes.

"I need you to take me to the nudie bar, Norman."

"What?!" Norman cranked around in his seat so he could look directly at Gertrude. "Why?"

"I can't explain, but I assure you it's for a good cause."

"Gertrude, that's not what the CAP bus is for. I can't take you to a *bar*."

"I've got two Washingtons that say you can," she said slyly, holding out two wrinkled, filthy one-dollar bills. Norman sighed, turned around, and put the van in drive.

As they drove around the loop, Gertrude saw two little eyes peering at her from the window of trailer number nine.

"You know, it *is* only ten o'clock. This isn't exactly a breakfast joint. They're not even going to be open."

"That's OK."

"It is?"

"Yep. Don't worry. It won't take me long. And you don't have to come in."

"Come in? Of course I'm not going to come in. And I'm not going to wait around outside the bar either. This job don't pay much, but I still don't want to get fired from it."

"Fine then," Gertrude said, sounding exasperated. "When I come out, I'll just wait by the door. Just drive around the block until you see me."

Norman laughed. "Lady, you're nuts." A few minutes later, Norman pulled up in front of Private Eyes. "If anyone asks, I'm going to tell them that I dropped you off at the thrift store," he said, nodding toward the consignment shop next door.

"Yeah, right. Like I'd be caught dead shopping in that highfalutin' place. Nothing thrifty about that joint, no there ain't." Gertrude slammed the van door as an exclamation point.

Norm just shook his head and drove away.

Of course, the bar was closed. Gertrude leaned on her walker with one hand and pounded on the front door with the other. No one answered. She knocked again. Still nothing. So she pounded continuously until someone answered. When the door opened, Gertrude was surprised. Her hand was also quite sore.

"Hello!" Gertrude said. "I'm looking for Lori. Have you seen her?"

"Don't know any Lori," the man said and tried to shut the door.

Gertrude picked up her walker and shoved one of its wheels into the opening.

The man opened the door. "Look, lady, I don't know you. I don't know Lori. I'm just the janitor."

"Oh good," Gertrude said, and pushed the door open. "I was afraid I was going to have to waste time talking to someone in charge. My name is Gertrude."

"Andy," a baffled Andy said.

"Nice to meet you," Gertrude said, and pushed past him into the bar.

"Look, your friend's not here! No one is here!" Andy spread his arms to indicate that he was the only thing to see.

"I know. I'm just looking for clues."

"Clues? Why, what happened?"

"I don't know. That's why I need clues. Lori is missing."

"Missing? Did you call the cops?"

"No, no police. I'll find her. I just need some clues."

"Lady, I don't think this is such a good—"

"It smells bad in here," she said, scrunching up her nose.

"Yeah, well, that's why I have a job."

"So that's where they do it?" She pointed a stubby finger at the tiny circular stage surrounding a single pole.

"Yeah. That's where they do it." Andy chuckled, but it sounded reluctant. "So, um, I have to get back to work, so can you ... like ... go or something? I'm pretty sure I wasn't supposed to let you in."

"Yep. I'll just be a minute." She looked at the bar. Then she walked around the bar and stepped behind it. She ran a finger along the top of it as if she was testing for dust. "It's sticky," she said, curling her top lip.

"Yep." Andy crossed his arms across his chest and sighed.

Gertrude bent over to look under the bar. "Is Lori a stripper?"

"What?"

18

She stood back up. "Is Lori a stripper?" she said slowly.

"I don't know," he said just as slowly. "I don't know Lori. I don't know anything except that I want to get you out of this bar."

"OK, just show me where the girls put on their costumes and whatnot, and I'll be out of here."

Andy sighed and headed toward the back. Gertrude followed him into a narrow hallway. Several open doors led to several small, empty rooms. "What are these?"

"Uh, those are for private dances and stuff."

"Oh," Gertrude said and quickly moved past them. They went by another door that said Do Not Enter. "What's in there?"

"The office."

"Do you clean the office?"

"Nope." Andy opened the door to a small room with gray walls. Gertrude stepped inside. There was a couch along one wall and a long counter along the other. Over the counter hung a long mirror. Various feathers and sequins were spangled on the floor. "Satisfied?" Andy said. "There's no one here."

Gertrude shuffled over to the mirror. The bar was littered with lotions, sprays, and various cosmetics. She shuddered when she spotted a Grace Space lipstick.

"You're right," she said, turning back toward the door. "I don't see any useful clues."

"OK then. Can you show yourself out?"

"Sure can." Gertrude headed for the door, still examining her surroundings as she went. When she reentered the big room, she marveled at how many tables and chairs there were. She hadn't realized Mattawooptock had that many "gentlemen."

She squinted as she stepped back out into the sunshine and was pleased to see Norman there waiting for her. She hoisted herself into the van and then pulled her walker in after her. "I thought you weren't going to wait."

"Well, truth be told, I was getting a little worried. You were in there a long time. I wasn't sure how much time someone could spend in a closed nightclub. Where we headed now, the liquor store?"

"Don't be silly. Back to the trailer park, Hoke!"

"Don't call me that."

"Yes, Norm."

3

Sophia opened the door before Gertrude could knock. "Did you find her?"

"Where is Tornado?"

"He's up there," she said, pointing to the top of the fridge.

"Oh good. No, I didn't find her. And I didn't find any leads yet. Maybe it is time to call the police."

"No, don't! Please don't!" Sophia cried. "Our mother said that if anyone finds out we're here alone, the cops will put us in foster care, and we'll get split up."

"Hmm. Well, I think that might be a slight exaggeration. All right, you guys watch television or something, and I'll look around here for some leads."

"We don't have cable."

"OK, well, then read a book."

"Carl can't read."

"Then read him a book! I'm trying to think here."

Gertrude went into the kitchen and looked around again. She spotted some unopened mail and picked it up. *This probably won't tell me anything, but it could be interesting*, she thought. Most of it was junk mail, but she did find a bank statement. She opened it and quickly learned that Lori could definitely afford a babysitter. Her statement showed regular five hundred dollar deposits. *She must be getting some serious tips!*

"Did you find anything?" Sophia reappeared.

"Nope," Gertrude said, shoving the statement under a brown envelope offering a fake key and promising a new car. "Now skedaddle! I'm trying to work here."

Sophia looked hurt, but she did leave. Gertrude took the statement back out. There wasn't much other activity. An occasional cash withdrawal and those mysterious giant deposits. Apparently, Lori didn't use a debit card and didn't write checks, at least not with this account. Gertrude looked around the top of the bar for other bank statements but didn't see any. She opened some drawers and rifled through them, but most of them were nearly empty. Gertrude could hardly stand the sight. So she gave up on the kitchen and meandered through the living room, looking around and wondering how anyone could live with so little stuff, and for that matter, why anyone *would* live with so little stuff when they had more than ten grand in checking.

Gertrude peeked into a small bedroom the kids apparently shared. Sophia was indeed reading to Carl. Gertrude moved on down the hall, past the bathroom and into the master bedroom. She found an unmade full-size bed and piles of clothes, which she looked over for feathers and sequins, but found none.

Something caught hold of her then, alone in this stranger's bedroom. It was like an itch she just had to scratch, a thirst she just had to quench, an irrepressible drive to figure this thing out. Suddenly, she was bitten by the mystery bug, and it had its teeth in deep.

She turned to her right and started with the first thing she saw, which was a vacuum cleaner. She took out the bag and emptied its contents onto the floor. She sifted through them meticulously and found absolutely nothing helpful. (She did find two Legos, which she set aside for Carl.) Then she moved onto the next thing to her left, which was a laundry hamper. Through the clothes she went, through every crease, every stain, every pocket. Nothing. No incriminating blood. No wads of cash. Nothing.

In this way, Gertrude went through the entire room, methodically and exhaustively. When she got to the bed, she shoved her short arms between the mattress and the box spring and felt around the length of the bed. Near the foot, her fingers grazed the edge of something that felt like paper. She couldn't quite get a hold of it though, so she stood up, turned around, and pushed at the mattress with her butt. It didn't move. She leaned forward, and then, pushing off her walker, she slammed her hind end into the mattress, and it slid off the box spring about eight inches. That would be enough. She reached in and grabbed what turned out to be a large, flat, brown envelope. She pulled it out and then hopped up onto the bed. She gingerly reached into the envelope and pulled out its contents ...

Yikes! Gertrude's hand flew over her eyes. Then she peeked out through her fingers. There were naked people. Two of them. And the man looked a lot like the owner of Mattawooptock's only water park.

She flipped the top picture over. Two more naked people underneath it. Same woman, who she was starting to assume was Lori. Different man, and she didn't recognize him.

Third photo. Same woman. Different man. Gertrude gasped. This man was none other than Lance Pouliot—the Mattawooptock Mayor. Mattawooptock's *married* mayor. Gertrude had seen his wife on the local news, and this *wasn't* her.

Deep in her soul, Gertrude held a special reserve of disdain for Lance Pouliot. A few years back, he had tried to burn down her church, which also served as a homeless shelter. Not only had he gotten away with it, he had gotten himself elected as mayor, in part by running on a platform that promised to shut down the town's homeless shelter, which of course, thus far he had failed to do.

She stared at the naked woman's face. *If this is Lori, she is a busy lady!*

24

Gertrude slid the photos back into their envelope, and then zipped the envelope into her walker pouch, a floral-patterned bag that hung off the front of her walker. It served as her handbag, and its contents were putting a significant strain on the pouch's seams.

She left the bedroom and called out, "Sophia? I've got to have to call the CAP bus again. You stay here and watch Tornado and Carl."

"Where are you going?"

Gertrude ignored her. She called for a ride and then walked back to stand in front of her trailer. It was just after noon and had turned out to be a beautiful day. Her stomach rumbled, and she realized she hadn't eaten anything lately. She rummaged around in her walker pouch until she found some yogurt-covered raisins and a breath mint. This would have to do for now. She was looking for a missing woman. Creature comforts could wait.

The van pulled up in front of her trailer, and Gertrude was dismayed to find that Norman's shift was over. He'd been replaced by Andrea, a power-tripping, by-the-book ex-librarian.

Gertrude climbed into the van and smiled at the man sitting in the back seat. "Hi, Tiny," she said.

He nodded.

"Where to?" Andrea asked.

Gertrude had to think fast. She needed to go to the water park, but she couldn't think of a way to make this sound like a necessity, especially since the water park was likely closed for the season.

"G's Automotives," Gertrude said and looked out the window.

"G's Automotives?" Andrea turned around and looked at Gertrude. "Why do you need to go there?"

"None of your business," Gertrude tried.

"It is my business!" Andrea waved a clipboard at Gertrude. "I have to log all your stops, and stops have to be necessary, or you don't get a ride. It's right in the rules!"

Gertrude looked her in the eye and tried to be a good liar. "Why else would someone go to see a mechanic, Andrea? I need to pick up my car. Then I won't need to ride around with you anymore!"

"You have a car?" Tiny said from the backseat. He sounded amazed.

Gertrude pressed her lips together and looked out the window.

4

G had his head under a hood when Gertrude walked in. She stood by his front counter, patiently waiting for him to notice she was there—for about two seconds. Then she loudly cleared her throat.

He looked up. "Oh, hey, Gertrude," he said, sounding less than excited to see her.

"I need your help," she said.

She wasn't sure, but she thought she saw him grimace.

He headed toward her, wiping his hands off on a rag. "Need help moving another cast iron clawfoot tub?" he asked.

She shook her head. "I don't think I have room for another one. I just need a ride to the water park."

"You mean the small, weird one just outside of town?" The "water park" was actually an average-sized pool surrounded by inflated slides and bouncy houses with hoses hooked up to them. And a few arcade games inside a small adjacent building. It was the kind of establishment that could only survive in a tiny, out-of-the-way town like Mattawooptock. In rural central Maine, the place was thriving.

Gertrude nodded.

"OK, can I ask why you need to visit a closed water park?"

"I need to talk to the guy who owns it."

"Silas?"

Gertrude shrugged. "I guess so."

"What do you want with Silas?"

"It's personal."

G stared at her for several seconds. It looked as if he was trying to figure her out. But then apparently he gave up because he sighed and said, "OK, fine. But does he live at the water park?"

"Yes," Gertrude said. She had no idea.

Gertrude followed G out to his truck. He opened the passenger door for her and then pulled a milk crate out of the bed of the truck. He flipped it over and placed it at her feet so she could climb into his truck. This was not the first time G had given Gertrude a ride.

About five miles and ten minutes later, G pulled into the empty parking lot of WaterWoopPark.

"I don't think he lives here, Gertrude. The place looks deserted."

Gertrude put her hand on the door handle. "Would you mind waiting for a few minutes?"

G looked at her incredulously. "Gertrude, there's no one here!"

"I know, I'm just going to have a look around."

G looked through the windshield at the tall wooden fence that encircled the park. "It's a closed building and a closed fence. I don't think there's much to see."

"I know. Can you help me out?"

G sighed. But he got out of the truck and walked around it to place the milk crate. He helped her out and then watched her walk toward the door. She pulled on the door handle. It was locked.

"Satisfied?" G asked from behind, still standing by his truck.

Gertrude looked up. "Can you feel the top of the doorframe, G?"

He came up and stood beside her, and then looked down at her skeptically. "You mean, feel for a key?"

"What else would I want you to feel for?"

"This is a business, Gertrude. He's not going to leave a key, even if this is Mattawooptock."

"Would you please do it? Or go get my crate so I can do it?"

G sighed again and halfheartedly reached up and felt the top of the frame. Then he held up his empty hand. "See? Nothing."

Gertrude stepped back and surveyed the scene in front of her.

G waited patiently for a minute and then asked, "Can we go?"

"There!" Gertrude triumphed, pointing at a rock pressed up against the building, several feet from the door.

"There what?"

"There. That rock."

"What rock?" G snapped. There were many rocks.

"That one," Gertrude said, without pointing. "It's different from the others."

G stared at the rocks at the base of the building. "I don't see it."

Gertrude heaved a frustrated sigh and took two steps toward the rock and pointed with her chin. "That one."

"So I guess you're expecting me to pick that rock up?"

She just looked at him.

He walked over to the building and bent to retrieve a rock.

"Not that one," Gertrude said, exasperated, "*that* one."

G picked up a different rock. "This isn't a rock," he said.

"I know. Flip it over."

He did. "I'll be darned," he said. There was a small compartment in the bottom of the false rock. He opened it, and removed a key.

30

"Gimmee," Gertrude said, holding her hand out toward him.

"No," G said, pulling it away from her eager clutch. "What are you going to do with it?"

"What do you think?"

G frowned. "You want to tell me why we're breaking into a water park?"

"We're not breaking in. We have the key."

"Gertrude! You said you had to talk to Silas. He's obviously not here. So let's go. The man probably has a telephone, you know."

"Fine!" Gertrude snapped. "Why don't you just leave. I can walk home."

G laughed. Gertrude never *walked* anywhere, let alone the five miles home. That would wear the tennis balls right off her walker. "I'm not leaving you here," G said. "But I need you to tell me what we're doing."

"We're just going to take a look around, make sure Silas isn't here."

"If he was here, wouldn't he have come to the door by now?"

"Not if he can't."

G furrowed his brow. "Is something wrong with Silas?"

"Don't know. You won't give me the key."

Looking exasperated, G walked to the door and unlocked it. Then, holding it open with one hand, he waved Gertrude in with the other. "Ladies first. Let's hope there's no alarm system."

"Yeah, right. Who would break into this place?" Gertrude asked as she entered the dark foyer. She immediately groped around the adjacent wall for a light switch.

"Hang on. I've got a flashlight on my phone," G said.

Her fingers found the switch. "No need for one of those fancy doohickeys."

"You're probably right," G said, following her inside. "If you had a cell, I'd probably have to go on a lot more of these errands."

"Oh, stop it. You know you love feeling needed."

G didn't respond.

"At least I'm not asking you to babysit my cats again.... What's that?" Gertrude asked.

"What?" G asked.

"That. The House of Balls."

"Um, it's a house of balls," G said.

"I can see that. I can read. But what is a house of balls?" Gertrude was downright excited.

"It's just a big box full of balls. For kids to play in."

"Oh goodie!" Gertrude exclaimed and rushed over to the ladder.

"Gertrude, don't get in there. I might not be able to get you out!" G hurried after her.

But she was already on the ladder. Then she froze. "Oh Mylanta!"

"What?" G asked, but then followed her gaze and started. There was a woman in the house of balls. And she appeared to be very dead. Her face was colorless, and her chest, which was eerily still, had a bright red circular stain on it. As G stared, Gertrude jumped into the house of balls.

"Gertrude, no!"

Gertrude landed and instantly sank to her shins. She tried to pick up one short leg, but then the other leg sank and she toppled over sideways with a small yelp. She flailed her arms, looking absurdly like a chubby Raggedy Ann doll and then sat up with a giant smile on her face. "This is great!" she exclaimed.

"Gertrude, get out of there! We need to call the police. And you're going to get yourself in trouble. Get out of there!"

"Oh, don't get your knickers in a bunch. I'll be right out. Just hang on a sec." Gertrude slogged over to the body and peered closely at it, looking for something, *anything*, to connect Lance Pouliot to this dead body.

"For the love of God, don't touch her!"

"It's not the woman from the photos."

"What photos?" G asked.

Gertrude felt around in the balls, searching for something, or someone, else.

"That's it. I'm calling the cops." G didn't have a signal, so he left Gertrude alone in the balls and went outside to call the police. When he returned, Gertrude had miraculously extracted herself and stood waiting for him.

"Are they coming?" she asked.

"Of course they're coming. There's a dead body."

"She's been shot," Gertrude informed him matter-of-factly.

"You didn't touch her, did you?"

"Of course not!" Gertrude said. "Don't be ridiculous."

They stood there together, awkwardly, silently, just inside the door, waiting to see some sign of life outside.

They heard it before they saw it. Sirens. Then, thirty seconds later, blue lights.

G greeted the lead officer by name. "Hale," he said, and nodded. They had played high school football together.

"G," Hale said, returning his nod. "You found the body?"

"Over there," G said, pointing to the house of balls.

"You didn't touch it?"

G shook his head.

"OK, wait right here. One of us—"

"I know who did it," Gertrude interrupted.

Hale turned to her expectantly.

Gertrude felt nervous all of a sudden, an emotion entirely unusual for her.

"Well? Are you going to share your theory?" Hale asked, obviously impatient and annoyed.

Gertrude took a deep breath. "It was the mayor."

And Hale actually laughed. From deep in his belly, he whooped with laughter, his ridicule echoing to all corners of WaterWoopPark. "And just why do you think it was the mayor?"

Gertrude felt her face flushing red, another experience she wasn't used to. She didn't know what to say.

"OK then," Hale said, regaining his professional demeanor, "you guys sit tight. One of us, probably me, will be back to take your statements." Hale walked over to the house of balls, took one look, and then spoke rapidly into his radio. Another policeman asked G and Gertrude to step outside, and then he began to wrap trees with caution tape.

G stood with arms crossed, constantly shifting his weight from one foot to the other. His jaw was tight, and he seemed unable to look at Gertrude. "The mayor?" he muttered through his teeth.

Gertrude didn't respond.

"I know none of us love the guy." (G also attended the church Lance Pouliot had tried to burn down.) "But I wouldn't be accusing him of murder to the cops. That could get you into trouble, Gert."

Gertrude heard him loud and clear, but she didn't respond. She was too angry.

Eventually, Hale returned. "Can I have your full names and addresses please?"

They gave him the info.

"So, what were you two doing here exactly?"

"I needed to talk to Silas, the owner," Gertrude said.

"About what?"

"None of your business."

Hale looked at Gertrude, surprised, then looked at G, and back to Gertrude. "Actually, this is a murder investigation, so it is absolutely my business."

"I wanted to sell him Girl Scout cookies," Gertrude said snippily.

Hale sighed. "Ma'am, lying to the police is against the law."

"No, it's not," she said.

Hale chewed on his lower lip. "OK, so you were here to talk to Silas. Then what happened? How did you get in?"

"We used the key."

"You had a key?"

"No, we found it."

"She found it," G said, pointing at Gertrude.

"OK. Found it where?" Hale asked.

"I have a cat named Hail."

"That's great. Where did you find the key?"

"In the hide-a-key rock," Gertrude said matter-of-factly. "Over there."

Hale looked. Then he looked at Gertrude as if he'd never seen such a thing. Then he wrote something in his notebook.

"Who is she?" Gertrude asked.

"We haven't made a positive ID yet," Hale said.

"So you have made an ID?" Gertrude asked.

"What?" Hale snapped, looking genuinely confused.

"You said you hadn't made a *positive* ID, which means you've made a less-than-positive one. Otherwise, you would have just said you didn't know."

G rolled his eyes and took a step back from Gertrude.

Hale sighed. "One of the guys thinks he recognizes her, thinks she's a local waitress. But we don't know anything for sure yet, so don't go telling everyone. Then anyone who knows a waitress will fly into a panic."

"Private Eyes?" Gertrude asked.

"What?" G said.

"How'd you know?" Hale asked.

"Lucky guess," Gertrude said. "I know how you cops like to hang out there. G, you need to get me home. Right now."

"Hang on," Hale said. "Not so fast. I have some questions for you."

"What?" Gertrude asked.

"How did you know she worked at Private Eyes?"

"I told you. Lucky guess."

"OK, so what did you want to see Silas about?"

"I told you. Girl Scout cookies."

"A-huh." Hale wrote something down in his notebook. "So you're the one who found the body?"

"Yep."

"And what made you look in the house of balls? Did you expect to find Silas in there, inside his locked, closed building?"

"Nope," Gertrude said, completely missing his sarcasm. "I just like balls."

Hale stifled a chuckle. "OK then. So you found the body. Then what did you do?"

"I jumped into the balls."

"You did what?"

"Oh, don't get all shook up. I didn't touch anything. I just wanted to make sure she was dead."

"Did you touch the body?"

"No, of course not. I watch television."

"So then how did you confirm that she was dead?"

"I could tell once I got close enough."

"But you didn't touch anything."

"I said that already."

Hale sighed again. Suddenly, he looked exhausted. "So did you see or hear anything suspicious?"

"Nope," Gertrude said.

"Nothing at all?"

"Nope."

"OK, well, we may need to fingerprint you later, so we can rule them out when we find them all over our crime scene."

"Oh yeah, like you're going to fingerprint an entire house of balls. What would that be, the print of every kid in Somerset County? That was a smart place to murder someone if you ask me," Gertrude said.

"Except that I didn't ask you," Hale said. Then he looked at G. "How about you? You see or hear anything useful?"

"No, sorry, man. Nothing. The place was still, dark, and quiet."

"And do you know what she wanted with Silas?" Hale asked.

"No, sorry."

"So you just drive her around?"

"Sometimes, yeah. Sometimes I have trouble saying no."

"OK then," Hale said and then looked at both of them as if he wasn't sure what to do next. "You can take her home. Please, you two, don't talk to anyone about this, especially reporters. And you," he said, looking at Gertrude, "don't leave town."

5

"Can't you drive any faster?"

"Why are you in such a hurry to get home, Gertrude?" G asked.

"It's time to feed the cats."

"Gertrude! The next time you come asking for my help, maybe I'll just say no!"

Gertrude looked at him, shocked. "Really?"

"Well, yeah. You keep lying to me!"

"No I don't."

G sighed as he pulled into the trailer park. "Well, are you at least going to be safe?"

"Yes. Although, do you have any guns?"

G laughed. "Yes, I have guns. And no, you're not getting anywhere near them. I can't think of a worse idea than Gertrude with a gun." He put the truck in park and then looked at her. "What's going on, Gert? What are you mixed up in?"

"Nothing. I just like guns. Can you help me out of the truck please? I need my crate."

G looked at her for another moment, as if trying to decide whether or not to let it go. Evidently he decided in favor of getting on with his day because he got out of the truck and circled around to help her out as well. As she climbed out, he looked around the trailer park as if he was looking for signs of danger. Gertrude saw this and felt guilty. "I'll be OK, G. Really. Thanks for your help."

"OK," G said, sounding reluctant. "You have a phone in your trailer?"

Gertrude nodded. "Several."

"I mean, do you have one hooked up, so you can call if you need help?"

"Yes, I'll call you if I'm in danger."

"No. Don't call me. Call 911."

"OK, 911. But if I'm in that much danger, all I have to do is pull on this thing." She reached down her shirt, and G drew back. Then he looked relieved when she pulled out a LifeRescue pendant. "Don't worry, G. I get into a pickle, I'll just press this button, and the cavalry will be on the way!"

G laughed then. "The *cavalry*? You mean an ambulance? You might want to call 911 too, so you get actual police. Just be careful, OK? Go snuggle your cats or organize your bottle cap collection, something safe," he said as he walked back around to his side of the truck.

"I don't collect bottle caps, G," Gertrude said and then muttered, "ridiculous" under her breath. As she watched him drive away, she took a few steps toward her trailer, but as soon as he was out of sight, she hurried to trailer number nine.

Gertrude banged on the trailer door and was surprised to hear an adult male voice call out, "Come in!" She had expected the door to be locked, which is how she'd left it. She opened the door and found a strange man standing over Sophia. He looked as if he was about to pick her up, and Gertrude flew into action. Screaming like a deranged banshee, she picked her walker up, held it out in front of her, and charged at him full speed ahead. Her walker hit him, knocking him off balance. He staggered two steps backward, trying to regain his balance, and ended up pinned against the wall by a walker. She leaned toward him. "Who are you, and what are you doing here?"

She thought she must seem pretty tough, so she wasn't pleased when the man laughed. He held his hands up. "I'm their dad! I'm their dad! It's OK."

Gertrude looked down at wide-eyed Sophia, who nodded her confirmation. Gertrude eased the walker off the man, put it back on the floor, and leaned on it. "Sorry."

The man stood up straight and smiled, rubbing the back of his neck. "It's OK. I guess. And just who are *you*?"

Gertrude cleared her throat and announced, "I'm Gertrude," as if that explained everything.

"She's our neighbor, Dad," Sophia said, sidling up to him. "She's nice ... sort of. She's been looking for our mother."

"Oh yeah? Did you find her?"

"Yes. She's dead."

The man's jaw dropped. "Wow, you're big on tact, aren't you?"

"Not really."

The man looked down at his daughter. "Sweetie, can you and Carl go pack your things?" Then to Gertrude he said, "I'm Joel."

Gertrude watched the kids walk down the narrow hallway. "Why aren't they crying?"

"Would you like to sit?" Joel asked, motioning toward the couch.

Gertrude shook her head.

"They're not crying because they're not sad. They hardly know Lori. She's mentally ill and refuses to stay on her medication, so she keeps getting in trouble with the law. She's been in and out of jail. I have custody. But a few months ago, Lori picked them up from a birthday party. Sophia says she told them that I didn't want them anymore and that they had go with her. Anyway, I've been looking for—"

"Did you kill her?" Gertrude interrupted. She just wanted to make sure.

"No! Of course not. I'm a mailman. I don't kill people. ... Why? Was she murdered?"

"Yes. But don't tell anyone. I wasn't supposed to tell anyone. Cops told me not to."

"Um, OK. So anyway, I'm going to take them home now. Thanks for trying to help them."

Joel headed down the hall toward the children, leaving Gertrude to find her own way out. She scooped Tornado off a windowsill and headed toward the door. She was almost there when there was a sharp knock. Hoping it wasn't the murderer, Gertrude peeked out the window to see a police car.

"Yeah?" Gertrude called.

"Somerset County Sheriff's Department."

"Yeah?" Gertrude repeated.

The door opened. "You again," Hale said.

"Why isn't anyone ever happy to see me?"

"What are you doing here?"

"I live here."

"You do?" Hale stepped into the trailer, uninvited.

"Well, yeah, in trailer number three."

"So what are you doing in this trailer?" Hale asked. Joel and the kids appeared behind her then. Each kid had a stuffed backpack on their shoulder. "And who are you?" Hale asked Joel.

"I'm Joel Hicks. These are my kids, Sophia and Carl."

"Kids, can you go wait in your rooms, please? I need to talk to the grown-ups," Hale said.

Sophia rolled her eyes. "We only have one room and we already know someone killed our mother."

Hale looked at Gertrude. "You know, if I can find a way to throw you in jail, I think I might."

"Does jail have cable?" Gertrude asked.

"So you knew who the body was back at the water park, and you didn't tell us?"

"I didn't know."

"You didn't know," Hale said, incredulous. "So it's just a coincidence we find you in the dead woman's trailer?"

"I was looking for my cat."

Hale looked stupefied. He took a step closer to her and almost growled, "Go home." Then he looked at the children and softened his voice, "Kids, please go to your room for a few minutes."

Sophia looked up at her father, who nodded. She rolled her eyes again and walked away. Carl followed like a loyal disciple. Gertrude didn't move. Neither did Tornado.

"So," Hale began, ignoring Gertrude as if he hoped that would make her go away. "Lori Hicks is your wife?"

"Sort of. She never actually took my name. Why, was she using my name now?"

"Apparently. Her employer has her as Lori Hicks."

"Her legal name is Norton. We were married eight years ago, but she left a few years later, shortly after Carl was born. Since then, she's had very little to do with the kids, but she grabbed 'em a few weeks ago. I've only just found them."

"And how did you?" Hale asked.

"How did I what?"

"Find them?"

"Oh, Lori called me late last night. Said someone had left her threatening notes. Told me to come get the kids. She sounded scared, so I left right away."

"Did she say who was after her?"

"Nope, and I didn't ask. Lori is always mixed up in something. I was just thinking about the kids."

"I understand that. So, do you know if Lori was involved with drugs?"

"Probably."

"And when you were together, what did she do for a living?"

"She worked in a flower shop."

"To your knowledge, did she ever do any erotic dancing?"

Joel chuckled dryly. "To my knowledge, no. She wasn't really much of a dancer."

"OK. And where do you live?"

"Toledo."

Hale looked up. "Toledo, *Ohio*?"

Joel nodded. "Is there another?"

"And your wife, or ex-wife, or whatever, brought her kids to *central Maine* to hide out?"

Joel shrugged. "She spent part of her childhood in Commack, so I guess she knows the area? I don't know. Look, most of what she does doesn't make much sense. I'm sorry that she's gone, but I'm also not surprised. And I know her death has nothing to do

47

with me and the kids, so I'd just like to get them home. They've missed a lot of school."

Hale nodded. "It's not that I'm not sympathetic, but we'll need you to stick around for a few days, just until we get some answers. I'll keep in touch though. Is it all right with you if we look around this place?"

Joel stepped back to allow Hale and his silent partner into the living room. "Sure, it's not my place."

"OK thanks. You might want to get your kids out of here then. I don't want to scare or upset them."

"Wait!" Gertrude said.

Hale didn't even try to hide his annoyance. "What?"

"I've already searched the place."

Hale and his partner laughed. "OK then. Well, we're going to give it another go. Why don't you and your cat go on home and take a break? I'm sure you're exhausted from all this investigating you've been doing." He smirked and walked away from her.

Gertrude stormed out of the trailer and down the wooden steps, all the while muttering under her breath, "Fine. I *won't* show you the naughty photos. Fine, I *won't* tell you Lori was a blackmailer. Fine, I *won't* help you solve this crime. I'll just do it *myself*."

6

Gertrude fed her cats and then made herself a tuna fish sandwich with extra pickles. There was just enough space at the kitchen table for a single plate, and it was there she sat, surrounded by stacks of treasures. She propped the top photo against a pile of L. L. Bean catalogs and stared at it as she chewed. *I need to talk to Silas*, she thought. *I need his alibi. Then I'll find the guy from the second photo and get his alibi too. But how do I find Silas? I don't know where he lives. I know!* She slapped the table, startling Sleet, who was curled up in a nearby box of scarves. *Old Man Crow has one of those computers that's online. You can look up just about anything on those things.*

Gertrude hurriedly finished her sandwich, giving a small piece of tuna to Sleet as an apology, and then headed for the door. Minutes later, she was pounding on Old Man Crow's screen door. But no one answered.

She pounded again. *Oh no, I can't handle another dead body today.* She cupped her hands over the window and peered inside. The inside of the trailer looked pristine. *What a weirdo.* She pounded again. Then she heard some commotion inside. Soon, the door opened. "What?"

"Why isn't anyone ever happy to see me?"

"What do you want?"

"Can I use your computer?"

"No," he said and shut the door in her face.

She pounded on it again. "Please!" she hollered through the door. "It's a matter of life and death!"

He opened the door again. "What?"

"I said it's a matter of life and death," she repeated.

"Whose?"

"Whose what?"

"Whose life or death?"

"Oh, will you just let me in, old man? The sooner you help me, the sooner I'll be out of your hair." She looked up at his balding head. "Or what's left of it anyway." She pushed past him and headed inside. "Smells good in here. What is that?"

"Hygiene."

She made a beeline for the small, neat computer desk. When she got there, she sat down with a grunt.

"Get up," he said. "Don't touch anything. What do you need? Pay a fine to animal control? I'll do it for you."

"OK, OK old man. Don't get your diaper twisted." She stood up.

"Who you callin' old? You're not exactly a young'un." He sat down. "Now what's this emergency?"

"I need an address for Silas LeBlanc."

Old Man Crow looked at her incredulously. "Silas?"

"Yeah."

"He's my great-nephew, on my late wife's side."

"Oh great, then you must know where he lives."

"Ayuh."

"So can you take me there?"

"No."

"Why not?"

"Don't want to."

"But I told you it was a matter of life and death!"

"Whose?"

Gertrude put her arms on her walker and leaned forward on them as she rubbed her temples. *How can this man be so exasperating?* "I need you to take me to Silas so I can talk to him about a dead stripper."

Old Man Crow stood up. "Well, why didn't you say so? I'll go get my coat."

A few minutes later, they were both in Old Man Crow's Cadillac and were headed into town. "So now that we're partners—" Gertrude began.

"We're not partners."

"Well, whatever, why do they call you Old Man Crow?"

"That's my name."

Gertrude looked at him. "Your mother named you Old Man?"

"Don't be foolish. My mother named me Calvin. Calvin Crow. I don't know why they call me Old Man Crow. The kids started doing it years back. The same ones who egged my trailer. Took me forever to scrub that egg off. It got into the cracks in the vinyl. Went through a dozen toothbrushes that fall."

Gertrude's eyes grew wide. "You cleaned the *outside* of your trailer with a *toothbrush*?"

"No, with a *dozen* toothbrushes."

"Ever think you might be a little obsessive?"

"At least I don't *collect* toothbrushes." Calvin pulled over to the side of the street and put the car in park.

"Is this it?"

"No, but look."

Gertrude followed his gaze and saw Hale's cruiser parked in a driveway just down the street from them. "Oh horsefeathers!"

"What's going on Gertrude? Why are the police at Silas's house?"

"I told you there was a dead stripper!"

"That doesn't explain why the cops are involved. Strippers die all the time, don't they? Just like the rest of us?"

"Well, this one was shot."

"Oh. Well now, don't you think that was an important detail?"

"Yeah."

"So what, do you think Silas did it? Is that what the cops think?"

"I don't know what the cops think. They've made it clear they don't want my help. No, I don't think Silas did it. He wouldn't have been stupid enough to leave the body in his own house of balls."

"House of what?"

"Shh, here they come." Gertrude slid down in the seat to hide her head from view, which means she slid down about six inches.

"OK, the cops are in their car. Now they're leaving. You still want to talk to Silas?"

"Of course," Gertrude whispered, pushing herself back up into the seat.

"You don't have to whisper. They can't hear you." Calvin eased the car back into the street, drove two hundred feet, and pulled into a short driveway. "Now you don't mention the stripper around the wife. She's a nice churchgoing lady."

"Deal." Gertrude hoisted herself out of the Cadillac and then wrestled her walker out of the back seat.

They didn't even have to knock. Silas met them at the door.

"Hey, Si!" Calvin said.

"Hey, Calvin, what a surprise, come on in, I guess. What brings you here?"

Calvin walked into the kitchen and promptly sat down. "Got a lady here who wants to talk to you. Is Joanie around?"

"No, she's at church, quilting club or some darn thing. What's this about?"

"I need to know if Lori Hicks was blackmailing you," Gertrude said.

Silas's mouth flew open.

"I'll take that as a yes."

Silas sat down. "Please don't tell anyone. I've got enough trouble. And I sure didn't kill her."

"I know that," Gertrude said comfortingly.

Silas didn't look comforted.

"How much?" Gertrude asked.

Silas looked at the ceiling, his face red. "I had to give her a thousand dollars a month, or she would tell my wife about my affair. And I couldn't let that happen. I love my wife. Had to tell her I got into trouble gambling. Otherwise, she'd wonder where more than half our income was going. And she was such a sweetheart about it. Made me feel even guiltier. She just can't find out, she can't."

"I understand," Gertrude said, even though she really didn't. "So, your mistress, what's her name?"

"No idea."

"You don't know her name?" Gertrude asked, appalled.

"We didn't talk much."

"Does she work at Private Eyes?"

"Ayuh. Won't catch me in there again."

"So you met her there?"

"Who, Lori or the stripper?" Calvin asked.

54

"Well, I meant the stripper, but wasn't Lori a stripper too?"

"Nah, Lori just waited tables." Silas rubbed his jaw as if it ached. "I mean, she was a mostly naked waitress, but she didn't get up on stage and dance, at least not that I saw."

"OK, so this other woman, the stripper with no name, you met her there too?"

"Yeah. Look, is this really necessary?" Silas asked.

"Yes, it is," Gertrude said indignantly. "Are you still seeing her?"

"No!" Silas cried. "I haven't seen her since that one time."

"Do you have an alibi for last night?" Gertrude asked.

"Yes, I was home alone with my wife."

"OK. Good."

"Why are you doing this?" Silas asked. "Why not just let the police handle it?"

Gertrude thought for a second. *That's a good question. I'm not sure I should tell Silas my mayor theory.* "Because Deputy Hale made me feel stupid, and now I'm going to prove I'm not." There. That seemed as good a reason as any.

"Well, I don't know who killed her. I'm just a weak and pathetic man who drinks too much. And look where it got me—giving all my money to this Lori woman."

"Well, she won't be taking your money anymore."

"Right," Silas said dryly. "Lucky me."

Gertrude was almost out the door when she thought of another question. "Was Lori blackmailing anyone else?"

"Don't know," Silas said. "But I didn't kill her, so she certainly ticked someone else off."

7

"You mind if we stop at the drugstore on our way home?" Calvin asked. "They're going to close soon, and I have to pick up a few prescriptions."

"Yeah, sure. We've got to kill some time anyway before the strip bar opens."

Calvin made a choking sound. "What?"

Gertrude looked at him. "Did you swallow a bone?"

"What?"

"Well, what else could be our next move?"

"*We* don't have a next move. *We* are not the police. I'm going to get my medications, go home, and have a TV dinner while watching *Bonanza*."

"How are you going to relax when there's a killer on the loose?"

"Gertrude, I don't know what's gotten into you, but this is not our job."

"I don't care!" Gertrude snapped. "You have to take me to the strip club before someone else gets hurt! If you don't take me, I will go by myself, and there will be nobody to protect me."

Calvin rolled his eyes. "I'm seventy-one years old, Gertrude. I'm not going to be much protection, and I've worked hard to maintain my perfect reputation all these years. I'm not going to blow it now by entering a den of sin."

Gertrude snorted.

"What?"

"Your *perfect* reputation. That's what. You're ridiculous."

"What do you mean?"

"I mean that you are a cranky old man, a real meanieface! You have no friends. You are uptight and stingy."

"Wow, and you're just the tact fairy aren't you?"

"What in tarnation is a tact fairy?"

Calvin sighed as he pulled into the drugstore's lot. He got out of the car as if to leave her in it, but she climbed out and trailed in after him.

She busied herself with the perfume testers as she reviewed the situation in her head. *By my count, four suspects: Silas the water park owner, who seems quite innocent, with his alibi and all; mystery man from second photo; Mayor Pouliot; and Joel the wonder dad. Hmm. Oh, wait, what about their wives? Maybe they'd be mad enough to …*

"Ready?" Calvin was standing there staring at her.

"Yep." She turned and followed him to the registers.

"You smell ridiculous," Calvin said.

"Thank you."

As they approached the registers, the two clerks were snickering furtively. Then Gertrude heard one of them say, "No really. Be careful or he'll report you. I'm not kidding."

Gertrude looked at Calvin to see if he'd heard too. Apparently he had because he said, "I only report people who don't do their jobs. Or little arrogant hussies like you who think all old people are deaf. For your information, I'm wearing a seven thousand dollar pair of hearing aids. And I can afford these hearing aids because I worked hard my whole life, you ungrateful snots!"

One of the young women rang Calvin up with trembling fingers while the other tried to keep a straight face.

Gertrude remained silent until they were outside. "Right," she said. "Your reputation is impeccable."

"Oh, close your trap!" Calvin said as he opened his door. "Get in the car before I leave you here."

Gertrude did as she was told, for once.

"You got any other stops you need to make?" Calvin asked.

"You mean other than Private Eyes?"

"Yeah. That's what I mean. It's five o'clock. Pretty sure there's not a lot of action on the pole just yet."

"How did you know there's a pole?" Gertrude raised an eyebrow.

"Oh, stop trying to be a super sleuth. Don't all strip clubs have poles?"

"I don't know. I've only been in one strip club in my life."

"Well, you're one ahead of me."

Gertrude and Calvin decided to have dinner together. She suggested Burger King because she had several coupons in her walker pouch. Some of them weren't even expired yet, she was sure of it. But Calvin said that fast food was for white trash. Gertrude suggested the fried chicken joint on the edge of town, but Calvin wrinkled his nose up. Last time he was there, the waitress had forgotten to refill his wine, he said. Gertrude didn't even know they served wine there. Finally, after driving a few laps around town, Calvin decided on the Honor House. He said he hadn't been there in years, which comforted Gertrude immensely. She hoped that meant no one would remember him.

Gertrude had never been to the Honor House, and when they walked in and she looked at the "specials" board, she understood why. "Um, Calvin?" she whispered. "I can't afford to eat here. Are you bonkers?"

"Well then, just get some soup or something."

A well-groomed woman behind a small bar asked if they had reservations.

Instead of just saying no, Calvin said, "Do we really need reservations for 5:30 on a weeknight?"

The woman smiled. "Right this way."

The Honor House was set up like an ordinary house, with small rooms offering three or four tables each. Gertrude squinted in the dim light and then sat down clumsily in the wooden chair the hostess pulled out for her. The hostess then deftly collapsed the walker and leaned it against the wall. "Your server will be right with you," she said with a smile, and then scurried off to be verbally abused by some other patron.

The server introduced himself as Antoine, and offered them a glass of house wine. Gertrude quickly said, "No thank you. No alcohol. We are fighting crime tonight." The well-trained server didn't flinch at this.

Calvin wordlessly slid his glass closer to the server, who poured two tablespoons of wine into the glass. Calvin swirled the wine around in the glass, appearing to examine it for floaties, then sniffed it, then tasted it, and then nodded what was apparently approval. Antoine filled the glass and said, "I'll give you a moment with the menus."

"What was that all about?" Gertrude asked.

"What?"

"Why did you sniff the wine?"

"Gracious, Gertrude, haven't you ever left the trailer park?" Calvin opened his menu.

Gertrude followed suit. "How can you read this?" she asked. "There's no light in here."

"You don't need to read it, do you? Aren't you just having soup?"

Gertrude closed her menu with a snap and crossed her arms across her chest, determined not to speak for the rest of the meal. She ended up with a twelve dollar cup of French onion soup. Calvin had the apricot mustard chicken. When they'd been there two hours and Gertrude had lost feeling in all of her right leg and most of her left, Calvin ordered the chocolate torte for dessert. Fifty minutes after that, they were done, and the check was brought. Calvin asked them to go back and create two different checks so there wouldn't "be any confusion."

Antoine brought back two separate checks, still not letting on whether he was as annoyed with their presence as he should have been. Gertrude began to dig through her walker pouch for dollar bills and loose change. She had counted out seven dollars when Calvin reminded her, "Don't forget to tip." She got to nine dollars before giving up.

"That's all I've got, Calvin."

Calvin rolled his eyes, scooped up her money, ripped her check from her hands and headed toward the door, leaving Gertrude to unfold her own walker, pull herself up onto her numb legs, and then stand there while the blood flowed back into her toes. As it did so, she surreptitiously put the salt and pepper shakers into her walker pouch.

By the time she got outside, Calvin was waiting for her with the car running. She collapsed into the front seat, suddenly exhausted.

"I suppose I have to pay for your Private Eyes cover charge too?" he asked.

8

It cost Calvin ten dollars and a good deal of pride to get them into Private Eyes. The bouncer at the door looked them up and down and then laughed aloud before motioning them inside.

"Well, at least it's dark," Calvin said. "Maybe no one will recognize me."

Gertrude followed him to a table tucked into the shadows of a back corner. She tried not to look at the stage, where a woman was twitching her way out of a camouflage bikini. Soon, they were approached by a woman holding a notepad. Gertrude was relieved to see that, though she was scantily clad, all her private parts were covered.

"Hey, Old Man Crow," she cooed.

Calvin groaned. "So much for anonymity."

"What can I get for you and your gal here?"

"She's not my gal, and I'll take a glass of Chianti."

"I'm sorry, what?" The server leaned in closer.

"Chianti?"

"I don't think we have that."

"Fine. Red wine. In a clean glass please."

Gertrude declined to order, and the woman sauntered off.

"Why does it have to be so loud?" Calvin half-shouted to Gertrude.

"So that men can't hear their conscience," Gertrude half-shouted back. She tried to look around the room for clues without actually seeing any breasts. It wasn't easy.

The server returned with Calvin's wine. "Sure you don't want anything, honey?"

It took Gertrude a moment to realize the woman was talking to her. "Uh yeah, sorry, running a little low on cash."

The woman gave up and moved on to the next table, which appeared to be full of high school boys. "They can't possibly be old enough to be in here," Gertrude said.

Calvin didn't respond.

She looked at him and was amused to find him apparently entranced by the avid hunter hanging off the pole. Gertrude scanned the room again, fearing that this little foray into Mattawooptock's underbelly was going to be in vain. Then she saw her. She stabbed a chubby elbow into Calvin's side.

"Ow!" he exclaimed, his hand flying to his side. "What was that for?"

"Look!" Gertrude hissed.

"Look at what?"

"That's her!"

"That's who?"

"The woman from the photos!"

"What photos?"

Oh yeah, I never showed him the photos. "I'm going to go talk to her. Drink your wine."

The woman was waiting on another table halfway across the room. Gertrude approached and then stood a few feet away, not wanting to interrupt the drink orders. The woman finished scribbling on her pad and then began to walk away when she noticed Gertrude staring at her. "Can I help you?"

"I like your dress," Gertrude said.

The woman took a step closer. She was wearing a low-cut neon green number that barely covered her hiney. "Well, thank you, honey. I like yours too." Gertrude was wearing a baggy, faded, flower-patterned romper that fell below her knees. She looked down at it in confusion. When she looked up, the woman was standing inches from her. She smelled like sandalwood and cigarette smoke.

"What's your name?" Gertrude asked, suddenly painfully aware of her discomfort. She fought the urge to step back from the woman.

"Trixie. What's yours?"

"Gertrude."

"And how can I help you tonight, Gertrude?"

"I have photos of you in bed with multiple men." Never has a smile faded so quickly. Trixie's eyes snapped to life. "Well, not at the same time," Gertrude clarified.

"Who are you?" she hissed.

"I'm not going to cause you any trouble," Gertrude said. "I'm just trying to figure out who killed Lori."

"Lori's dead?"

"Quite."

"Come with me," she said and headed toward the back. Gertrude followed. Trixie entered one of the little rooms, and Gertrude panicked at the thought that Trixie was going to give her a lap dance. Gertrude stepped into the room just enough so that the door would shut. Then she stood there. "You can sit," Trixie said.

Gertrude shook her head.

"So what happened?" Trixie crossed her arms.

"She was murdered."

"How?"

"Not sure."

Trixie began to pace. "That's too bad. Lori was a nice lady."

"You knew her well?" Gertrude asked.

"Not really. We just worked together."

"Did you do anything else together?"

"What's that supposed to mean?" Trixie snapped.

"Well, I have reason to believe that she was blackmailing some people. I just wondered if you were involved in that."

Trixie stared at Gertrude for several seconds, seeming to size her up. Then she said, "Do the cops know?"

Gertrude said, "I don't think so." Then she had a second thought. "But I did tell a friend, you know, for my own safety."

"So why are you making this your problem?"

"I have my reasons," Gertrude said.

"Well, you should be careful," Trixie said. "Lori was mixed up with some not-so-nice folks. Turns out people don't like being blackmailed."

"Were you in on it?"

"Just between us?" Trixie asked.

Gertrude nodded.

"Yeah, but I'll deny it. Besides, I'm sure the whole thing's over now."

"What was your cut?" Gertrude asked.

"Half."

"How many men?"

"Two."

"Who?" Gertrude probed.

Trixie didn't answer.

"Look, I know one of them was Silas."

Trixie became furious, and she looked scared. "I think I've answered enough of your questions. You're not even a cop. If you'll excuse me, I need to get back to work." She flung open the door and walked out.

When Gertrude came out onto the main floor, she saw Calvin staring at her. He actually looked concerned. She headed his way until something else caught her eye. The man from the second photo was sitting in front of the stage. He was alone. Gertrude veered off her path and headed his way. Before she could reach him though, Calvin grabbed her arm. "We should go."

"No, wait!" Gertrude cried as Calvin dragged her away.

"Come on. We've got to get out of here."

Gertrude gave up and followed Calvin outside. Once they were breathing the refreshingly clean outside air, Gertrude snapped, "What?! Now you'll probably have to pay to get us back in there."

"I'm not going back in there, you nincompoop!"

"Oh, name calling, nice."

Calvin headed toward his car. Gertrude looked around for a better plan and then followed him.

When they reached the Cadillac, Gertrude caught her breath and asked, "What happened?"

Calvin looked pretty winded himself. He put his arms on the roof of the car and leaned on them. "I'm too old for this, Gertrude. I'm glad you're having an adventure, but I don't want to be part of it anymore. That guy you were going to talk to? He's a cop. I know him. He used to date my daughter."

"You have a daughter?" Gertrude interrupted. She couldn't picture it.

"Yes, I have a daughter. Anyway, that guy's Frank Malone. First of all, he's married. Second, he's a cop, and you were going to ask him about a murder, and you're not a cop. You were going to get yourself in trouble, and that was going to call attention to me, and I couldn't let that happen, because you know who else was in that room?"

"Half of Mattawooptock?"

"My granddaughter!"

"You have a granddaughter?" Calvin was just full of surprises.

"Yes, she just took the stage, so to speak. Can you even imagine how uncomfortable that would have been if she had seen me in there, seeing her? Look, get in the car or don't. Either way, I'm going home. It's the middle of the night for crying out loud."

Gertrude got in the car. Calvin pulled out into the empty street.

"Calvin?"

He sighed. "What."

"I understand. You're tired. This isn't your adventure. But I think someone might be in danger. Would you help me make sure she's OK? You don't even have to get out of the—"

"No. If someone is in danger, tell the police."

"Pull the car over."

"What?"

"Pull over. I have to show you something."

Calvin pulled over. Gertrude unbuckled and then grunted as she rolled over to reach over the back of the seat to her walker pouch. She couldn't quite reach, so she pulled herself up and over the seat, causing her rear end to hover perilously close to Calvin's face.

"Do you mind?" he asked, pressing himself against his door.

She grabbed the envelope and allowed herself to drop back into her seat, which shook the whole car. She pulled the photos out of the envelope. Calvin flicked on the reading light and then gasped at the sight of Silas tangled up with Trixie. "This is the girl I was talking to. Trixie. I think she's in danger," she said, pointing to the top photo. Then she slid it off the pile. "And this," she said, pointing to the second man, "is your cop. I think Lori and Trixie were blackmailing these men with these photos. I found them in Lori's trailer."

"The men or the photos?"

"The photos. And Trixie said they were only blackmailing two men. Which means they hadn't started blackmailing one of them yet. I think they just started to blackmail the mayor, and he freaked out and killed Lori. I think he might kill Trixie too."

"Wait, why would Frank be in the strip club if he were being blackmailed?"

"I don't know," Gertrude said thoughtfully. "Maybe his wife allows him to go to the strip club but she draws the line at fornicating with the stripper."

"So," Calvin thought, "you're saying the mayor *framed* the water park owner?"

72

"Why not? He's a good suspect, being blackmailed himself and all. But we need to get the cop's alibi, to prove he didn't do it. The mayor will probably try to frame him for Trixie's murder! Time is of the essence, Calvin!"

Calvin rolled his eyes. "Have you shown the police these photos?"

"Yes," Gertrude lied. "The police don't care about a murdered stripper. It's up to us to protect these women!"

"I don't know," Calvin said thoughtfully.

Oh goodie, he's considering it. "Let's just stick with her for a little while," Gertrude said. "She won't even know we're there. Then, if she gets into real trouble, we'll call the police."

"No, Gertrude. I'm sorry. I'm drawing the line. If you think she's in danger, call the police now. I'm old. I'm tired. I'm going home and going to bed."

"Fine," Gertrude said and started to get out of the car.

"Wait," Calvin said.

Gertrude stopped and looked at him expectantly.

"I'm not going to just leave you in front of a bar at midnight. Let me take you home."

"No," she said and started to climb out again.

"If you don't let me take you home, *I* will call the cops and tell them you're mentally ill and you need help."

Gertrude gasped. "You wouldn't."

"I will."

Gertrude shut the door and slumped in her seat, defeated. "Fine. Take me home."

Truth be told, she was exhausted too. And she was nearly asleep when Calvin pulled into the trailer park.

"Did you know your granddaughter was a stripper?" Gertrude asked. She couldn't help herself.

"No, I most certainly did not," he said, pulling into his driveway.

Gertrude thanked Calvin for his help and then headed toward her trailer. She considered revisiting Joel, but all the lights were off in trailer number nine. And she was just too tired. So she took a hot bath, made herself some tea, and then crawled into a bed full of cats. *What a full day*, she thought as they purred her to sleep.

9

Gertrude awoke with a start. With her gaggle of cats, she was used to noises in the night, but this one was different. This noise didn't belong. She sat up and tried to peer into the darkness. As she quietly extracted herself from the bed, she heard a mighty crash followed quickly by what sounded like a female whimper. This emboldened her. She eased her bedroom door closed a few inches (that was all the give it had) and reached behind it for one of her baseball bats. She'd been collecting them at yard sales for years, just for such an occasion as this. She wrapped her fingers around the first bat they touched and, pushing walker in front and dragging bat behind, she entered the narrow hallway that led toward the noise. When she entered the living room, she saw a flurry of motion and then heard her own front door shut. Assuming the intruder had left, she flipped on the light to confirm and proudly noted that a box of slinkies had slid off its perch and landed upside down in the path, apparently close enough to the criminal to cause a fright.

Gertrude picked up the slinkies and then surveyed the room to see if anything was missing. It didn't appear there was. She gingerly approached the door, and then ripped it open to peer outside, but there was no longer anything to see. She shut, and locked, the door. *Guess I'm going to have to start locking this, now that I'm fighting crime.*

Gertrude went back to bed, but had some trouble falling back asleep. *The prowler was probably looking for the photos. But who knows I have the photos? Just Calvin and Trixie. Calvin doesn't want the photos, for sure. So it must have been Trixie. But why does she want them? Oh, of course! She's going to take over the blackmailing! Why, that little vixen!*

Gertrude bounced out of bed the next morning, nearly landing on Hail's tail, and quickly got herself presentable enough to scoot over to Old Man Crow's trailer. A little voice in her head whispered that he might not be happy to see her so early, so she made him some coffee and poured it into a travel mug she'd gotten at Goodwill. It said "Little River Casino Resort, Manistee, Michigan" on it. She thought he would like it. She grabbed a few of her many flavored cream cups—

she thought he seemed like an Irish Cream kind of guy—and a few Splenda and sugar packets and headed out the door. It was difficult to walk like this, so she took her time, balancing the travel mug on top of the walker handle with her left hand, and wondering if she might be able to find a walker cup holder at a yard sale.

Eventually, she reached the trailer and rapped on his door. Of course, he didn't answer. She shivered in the early morning chill and pounded again. "Let me in, Calvin! It's cold out here."

"It's probably downright toasty back in your own trailer!" Calvin called.

She pounded again. "Let me in! I have exciting news! Some crook broke into my trailer last night!"

Calvin immediately opened the door. Was that actual concern she saw on his face? "Are you all right?"

"You betcha!" Gertrude said, shoving the coffee at his chest and pushing her way past him. "I brought you creamer and an assortment of sweeteners. Now drink up! We have work to do." She was both amused and disappointed to see that Calvin was still in his housecoat.

Calvin rolled his eyes. But he did pick up two sugar packets. "So what happened with the intruder?"

"Nothing. She broke in, I'm guessing to steal the photos. But she didn't get them, no siree, and I chased her out of the trailer with a bat."

Calvin gave her a long look, apparently processing. Then he smirked, "You sure she wasn't after your salt and pepper shaker collection?"

Gertrude frowned. "How do you know I collect salt and pepper shakers?"

Calvin shrugged. "Doesn't everyone?" He took a sip of his coffee. "Mmmm, not bad, Gert."

"Don't call me Gert."

"So you sure it was a she? You got a good look at her?"

"No, didn't see her at all. But it had to have been Trixie. Who else could it have been?"

"You chased her out of the trailer with a bat, but you didn't see her?"

"It was dark," Gertrude sassed. "Besides, like I said, it was Trixie."

"That's a fair bit of conjecture, there, Gert."

"I don't know what that means. I said, don't call me Gert. Go get dressed."

"Why do I have to get dressed?"

"We have to go see Trixie!"

"*We?* Why do I have to go?"

Gertrude really just wanted his car, but she didn't want to hurt his feelings. "I need you. You're my partner."

Calvin appeared to be thinking about it. "Fine. But only because I don't have anything else to do." He picked up his coffee and headed toward the bedroom. Gertrude watched his butt as he went. Then she picked up the unused cream cups and Splenda packets and dropped them into her walker pouch.

When Calvin returned with comb over in place and freshly pressed pants, Gertrude was standing beside his computer. "What?" he asked reflexively.

"Can we get where Trixie lives on this thing?"

Calvin guffawed. "I don't think 'Trixie' is even Trixie's real name."

"Why not?"

"I don't know," Calvin said, sitting down to dress his feet, "but if I were a stripper, I wouldn't use my real name."

"Oh horsefeathers!" Gertrude exclaimed. "How are we going to find out where she lives if we don't even know her real name?"

"Maybe we just wait till she goes back to work?"

"No!" Gertrude cried, indignant. "The mayor could kill her by then!"

"OK," Calvin said, scratching his chin, thinking.

"I know!" Gertrude said. "I bet they've got paperwork for their dancers at Private Eyes. Don't people have to fill out forms when they work somewhere?"

"You mean a W-4?"

"OK."

"And how are we going to get into Private Eyes to peruse their paperwork?" Calvin asked.

"The janitor will let me in. He's a good friend of mine."

"I think the politically correct term is custodian."

"Political shmitical," Gertrude said. "We don't have time for that nonsense. You'd better grab a coat. It's chilly out."

"You don't have one," Calvin observed.

"I know. That's why you're going to stop at my place so I can get one."

"Stop at your place? It's a hundred yards away!"

"Do you know how hard it is for me to walk with my disability?"

"What exactly *is* your disability?" Calvin asked.

Gertrude stopped in front of the passenger door, waiting for him to open it. "That's not a politically correct question."

10

Gertrude didn't have to pound on the door of the closed gentlemen's club for nearly as long this morning. Andy opened it after only a few thumps. "Fantastic," he said, heavy on the irony, and stepped aside to let Gertrude and her walker through.

"Finally! Someone's happy to see me," Gertrude said, entirely missing his sarcasm. "So, what do we know?"

Andy laughed. "You are turning into quite the gumshoe, aren't you?"

Gertrude smiled. She liked the word gumshoe. It had a funny ring to it.

Andy continued, "So your friend …" He paused to light a cigarette, then took a drag and leaned back on the wall as he exhaled. "She the one they found out at the water park?"

"Yes," Gertrude said, looking around, "and it wasn't *they*. It was *me*. *I* found her at the water park."

"Ah, I see. So what are you doing here now?"

"Looking for Trixie."

Andy laughed again. "Trixie, huh? Did you check the water park?"

Gertrude's head snapped around. "No, why? Do you think she's there?"

Andy held up both hands. "No man, I'm just messing with you. I don't know who or where Trixie is. I told you, I'm just the janitor."

"Cambodian," Gertrude tried to correct him.

"What?"

"The politically correct term is Cambodian."

Andy just stared at her.

"So, have you found any clues as you've been cleaning up?"

"No, sorry. Just the usual."

"What's the usual?"

Andy grimaced. "You don't want to know."

"Fine. Well, can you look the other way so I can go rummage through the office?"

He laughed again. "No!"

Gertrude reached into her walker pouch and found a crumpled dollar. She smoothed it out and handed it to him.

He took it gingerly. "What's this supposed to be?"

"It's a bribe, silly. See ya!" And she was off. But alas, Andy followed her all the way to the office.

"What are you looking for?"

She didn't answer him at first. But then she saw what she was looking for. "Aha!" she said, grabbing the folder marked "W-4s." "Just need some information about Trixie, like her home address."

"Ah, I see. So you're just going to walk up to this stripper's place and pound on the door all by yourself?"

"I won't be alone. I have Calvin."

"Who's Calvin?"

"My assistant."

"You have an assistant? How much does that gig pay?"

"I'll show myself out," Gertrude said and headed for the door.

"Hey, you can't just take the folder!"

"Watch me!" she said without turning around.

"No! What if someone sees it's missing?"

Gertrude wheeled around. "No one is going to see that it's missing. Look at all this junk! Total mess in here. If someone looks for it, which they won't, but if they do, they will just assume it's been misplaced. I'll bring it back eventually. Sneak it right back in, easy peasy."

"Something tells me nothing is easy with you," Andy said as Gertrude headed to the door.

"That was quick," Calvin said when Gertrude got in the car.

"I can be pretty speedy when I want to be."

"Wow, I'm impressed! You actually found a W-4 folder," he said, looking at Gertrude's hands. "Is there a Trixie in there?"

She opened the folder and flipped through the pages. "Oh horsefeathers. No, no Trixie. But there aren't that many employees. Let's just go to each of their houses and knock on their doors. Trixie is bound to answer one of them."

"Wouldn't it be a lot easier to just check their social media profiles?" Calvin asked.

"Social media?"

Calvin groaned. "Let's go back to my place."

Calvin typed each name into Facebook, and they were able to narrow their possibilities down to three names. Only three names didn't have an adult face as a profile picture. So Trixie was either represented to the social media world by a chubby toddler, a double rainbow, or a gray tabby.

"Nice cat!" Gertrude exclaimed. "I hope that one's Trixie."

Calvin grunted getting up. "Well, let's go find out. What's the first address?"

Gertrude looked at the W-4. "First stop: 13 Cemetery Road."

"Oh sure," Calvin said, "that's not foreboding at all."

"Really?" Gertrude asked with complete seriousness. "I kind of thought it was."

A few minutes later, Calvin pulled his Cadillac into a short dirt driveway. He put the car in park, and they both looked up at the neat white saltbox with green shutters.

"Quaint," Gertrude said.

"Not what were you expecting?"

"Nope. Thought I'd find something a little more … seedy?"

"Well, sorry you're disappointed," Calvin said. "So, are we going to just sit here?"

"Nope, let's go see if," she looked down at the paper, "Ashley has a gray tabby."

"We're still looking for Trixie, right?" Calvin asked. "Not the cat?"

"We can do both," Gertrude said.

Gertrude and Calvin approached the door shyly. "Wow, she even has a doorbell." Gertrude pressed the button.

Nothing.

They waited a minute. "Should I ring again?" Gertrude asked.

"No, it's possible no one is home. I think most people leave their house more often than we do."

"Wish I had a card or something to leave," Gertrude said.

"You mean like a business card?"

Gertrude started back to the car. "Yeah, like with my name and number."

Calvin chuckled, but Gertrude didn't know what was funny. "So what's the next address?" Calvin asked as he climbed back into the car.

She didn't answer for several seconds, as it was quite a process to wrestle her walker into the back seat and herself into the front. Finally, she managed, and she gave him a dirty look for not helping. He didn't seem to notice. She opened the folder and answered, "Twelve Hope Ave."

"OK. Where's that?"

"No idea. We could stop and ask for directions?"

"Nah, it's a small town. Let's just find it."

Twenty minutes later, they pulled into the parking lot of an apartment building that had definitely seen better days.

"Uh-oh," Calvin said.

"Afraid the roof's going to fall in on us?" Gertrude asked.

"No, just wondering which apartment it is."

Gertrude rechecked Jessica's W-4, but there was no apartment number. "Guess we just start with number one?" Gertrude said.

Calvin groaned. "I really hope no one shoots me. I don't want to die on Hope Avenue. That's just too much irony for me."

"Come on, ya big crybaby." Gertrude slammed the car door and headed to the first apartment door. She knocked. The whole door shook.

A man in a sort-of white tank top answered the door. "Oh no," he said.

"Andy!" Gertrude exclaimed. Then she looked at Calvin. "This is my Cambodian friend I was telling you about."

Calvin, obviously confused, stared at Andy.

Andy, with his pale, freckled skin and bright red hair, stared back, equally confused. "What are you doing here?" Andy asked.

"I'm looking for Jessica. Does she live with you?"

"Apartment four," he said and slammed the door.

"Friendly lad," Calvin said.

The two began to climb the stairs to apartment four. Gertrude went first and her walker slowed them down significantly.

"Give me that thing," Calvin grumbled.

"No."

"Yes. I will leave it right here behind us, and you can use the railings to lean on."

"Don't be foolish. These railings would give way with one good sneeze. Just hold your horses." And up they went. Finally, with Gertrude out of breath and Calvin out of patience, they reached their destination and Gertrude knocked.

A woman with a familiar-looking chubby toddler on her hip answered the door. "Yeah?"

"Are you Jessica?"

"Yeah?"

"OK thanks," Gertrude said and turned to go.

Calvin caught her by the arm. "Wait," he said. Then he looked at Jessica. "Did you know Lori Hicks?"

Jessica took her hand off the doorknob and protectively brought it to the toddler's back. "Yeah."

"Well, this here is Gertrude, and I'm Calvin, and well, Lori was a friend of Gertrude's, and we're just trying to figure out what happened to her. Might you have time to answer a few questions?"

Jessica nodded. "Come on in." She turned from the door and walked into a living room strewn with toys. Gertrude gave Calvin an incredulous look; he just smirked. Jessica lowered her son into a playpen. He immediately protested. She pulled a sippy cup out from between two couch cushions. "Have a seat," she said and sat in a lopsided glider that faced the couch.

"Thank you," Calvin said, and sat. Gertrude followed his lead.

"So, I'm not sure what help I can be. I didn't know her well. She was new."

"Did you know she was blackmailing folks?" Gertrude blurted out. Calvin elbowed her in the ribs. "Ow! What was that for?"

Jessica kept glancing back and forth between them, as if she couldn't quite believe what she was seeing. "Well, uh, no, I hadn't heard that. But I guess it doesn't really shock me."

"Why's that?" Calvin asked.

"I don't know. I guess she just kind of rubbed me the wrong way. She never really tried to be friendly with the rest of the girls, kind of acted like she was better than us, which is kind of ridiculous. If you're serving shots of Black Velvet while wearing black velvet pasties, you are *not* better than me."

Calvin's face turned varying shades of red.

"Was she friendly with Trixie?" Gertrude asked.

Jessica thought for a second. "Not that I know of."

"Is Trixie's real name Shannon or Abby?" Gertrude asked. (Double rainbow or gray tabby.)

Jessica hesitated. "Are you guys like some kind of elderly creepers?"

"Don't be foolish," Gertrude said. "I'm not elderly."

Calvin rolled his eyes. "No, we are not creepers. We would just like to talk to Trixie too."

Jessica still hesitated. "Well, it's sort of a code, you know, that we don't give out personal information about each other?"

"Look," Gertrude barked. She grabbed for her walker and pulled herself up. "We have reason to believe that Trixie was also blackmailing people, and we think that whoever killed Lori might also kill Trixie. We want to warn her. But if you don't want to help ..." she headed toward the door.

"Wait. OK. But I really don't think Trixie would blackmail anyone. Are you sure she's involved?"

Calvin and Gertrude spoke at the same exact time: "No" and "Absolutely," respectively.

Again, Jessica's eyes darted back and forth from one face to the other.

"What makes you think Trixie wasn't involved in the blackmailing?" Calvin asked softly, and, Gertrude noted, grandfatherly.

"Well, she's just not that ..."

"Evil?" Gertrude guessed.

"Smart," Jessica said.

"Ah, OK then," Calvin said and headed toward the door. "We may be wrong. Thank you so much for your time."

They were almost to the door when Jessica said, "Her real name is Abby. And if she is involved in this blackmail scheme, I'd be willing to bet she's just following Lori's lead."

Calvin turned back and smiled. "Thank you, Jessica. We appreciate your help. You and your little one have a nice day."

Gertrude thought her head might explode, but she waited until they were back in the car and backing out of the driveway before she spoke. "What was that?"

"What was what?"

"I have never heard you be that nice to anyone— ever. I didn't even know it was possible for you to be that nice!"

"Have you ever heard the saying 'you get more flies with honey than you do with vinegar'?"

"No one says that. Flies love vinegar."

"Fine. Whatever. My point is that your bulldozer approach wasn't working, so I thought I'd try kindness. Now, where does Miss Abby live?"

Gertrude took the folder off the dashboard and flipped through the W-4s. "27A Poplar Street."

"OK," Calvin said, making a left turn. Calvin knew the way to Poplar and soon pulled up in front of an old house turned duplex.

"Here we go," Gertrude said and grunted as she pulled herself out of the car. Her legs were getting mighty tired, but she wasn't going to admit it.

She knocked on the door. No one answered.

"There's no car in the drive," Calvin said.

"I can see that," Gertrude snapped. "Should we walk around and peek in the windows? See what we can see?"

"Absolutely not! She has neighbors. You really want the cops to show up and ask why we're playing peeping tom at a stripper's house?"

"Fine. Then what do you suggest?" Gertrude said, really wishing she could find a better partner.

"How about some lunch?"

"Not the Honor House again?"

"Let's do Thai food instead. My treat."

Gertrude looked at him suspiciously. "Why?"

"Haven't you heard the saying 'don't look a gift horse in the mouth'?"

"No one says that. What in tarnation is a gift horse?"

Calvin sighed and climbed back into his car.

A few minutes later, they were seated inside a Thai restaurant and Gertrude was trying to make sense of the menu. She looked up in a panic. "They serve *lard* here?"

"What?"

"It costs ten bucks for a plate of lard! That's gross!"

Calvin squinted at his menu. Then he whispered, "That's *larb*."

"Oh," she whispered back. "What's larb?"

"I don't know, but it's not pig fat. Just order something you recognize."

"I don't recognize any of this!"

The server approached. "Are you ready to order?" she said with a smile.

Calvin gave Gertrude a questioning look. Even though she wasn't ready to order, she nodded, thinking *I do better under pressure*. When it was her turn she said, "I'll have the spicy crispy duck, please."

"Yes, ma'am, how many stars would you like?"

"How many what?"

"Stars?" the server repeated.

"I dunno. How many are there?"

"No wait," Calvin tried, but Gertrude shushed him.

"I can order my own food, Calvin! Just because I don't speak Thai doesn't mean I can't order my own food!" Then, satisfied, she repeated her question, "How many stars are there?"

"Five," the server said, suddenly looking a little nervous.

"Then I'll have five, thank you very much," Gertrude said and snapped the menu shut for emphasis.

"And, uh, could we get an extra pitcher of water for the table?" Calvin asked with a smile.

The server nodded and scurried off.

"There it is again," Gertrude said.

"There what is?"

"Your fake nice voice. We'll have to come up with a name for it."

"It's called tact, Gertrude."

"No, that's not a catchy name. I'm going to call it your grampa voice."

11

"I'm dying," Gertrude said.

"I tried to stop you," Calvin said.

"You did not. What am I going to do? There's got to be a way to make the burning stop."

"Yeah—don't eat fire."

"I had to eat it, just to prove to you I could!" Gertrude reclined the seat with a thump.

"Easy! Do you know how much this car cost?" He pulled into a lot and Gertrude sat up enough so she could see where they were.

"What are we doing here?" she asked.

"Sit tight. I'm going to get you some Pepto."

Calvin was back in a few minutes with a bottle of pink magic. Gertrude frantically peeled the plastic off, opened the cap, and tipped her back. "Easy!" Calvin exclaimed. "I'm not sure it's possible to overdose on

Pepto, but I really don't want to be the one who has to deal with you if you do."

She slugged half the bottle, and then let out an unladylike belch. "Excuse me," she said, and screwed the cap back on.

"Better?" he asked.

"Not sure yet."

"Do we need to get you home?"

"Nope. I'm OK."

"All right. So where to next?"

"I don't know. Private Eyes eventually, but they're not open yet. I want to find Trixie-Abby, but I have no idea where to look."

"How about we go get you a cell phone?" Calvin said.

"Why?"

"Why? Because everyone else has one."

"You don't," Gertrude pointed out.

"I know, but you said you wanted to leave your card. Don't you want a cell phone number to put on that card?"

"Oh, good point."

"Plus, then we'd have a GPS so we don't have to spend so much time driving around in circles."

She eyed him suspiciously. "*That's* why you want me to get a cellular phone. You know, they make a thing called *maps*. And those are cheaper. Free even if we go get the ones at my house. I have an atlas for every state except Connecticut."

"Why Connecticut?"

"What do you mean?" Gertrude asked.

"I mean, you have an atlas for Hawaii and Alaska and not Connecticut? Is there a reason?"

"Why on earth would I ever go to Connecticut?" she said. Wasn't that reason enough? "Besides I can't afford a cellular phone. Don't be foolish."

"I'm pretty sure you can get one for no money down. You just need to sign a contract."

Gertrude narrowed her eyes. "A contract, huh? And just how much does *that* cost?"

Calvin sighed. "How about we just go look? We've got to kill some time."

"Fine."

When Calvin pulled into the parking lot of AmeriCell, Gertrude had to admit: she *was* excited. It had never occurred to her that she needed a cell phone, but now that she was here, she was pretty sure she wouldn't leave without one. Or three.

They entered the store, and a person who hadn't been blessed with a personality put Gertrude's name on a list. "Someone will be right with you," he said, without making eye contact.

Gertrude wandered toward a shiny display of tablets.

"No," Calvin said firmly. "Over here."

Gertrude followed him to a display of smart phones. "These only cost a penny?" she asked, her eyes growing wide.

"Like I said—contract. They're a penny today, real money tomorrow."

Gertrude handled every single phone in the room and then moved on to accessories. Calvin looked at his watch. "I know we needed to kill time, but this is ridiculous. Maybe we should go to a different carrier. Apparently these people don't care about customer service."

As if on cue, a young woman with blue hair approached them. "Good afternoon! How can I help you today?"

"Why is your hair blue?" Calvin asked. "Doesn't inspire a lot of confidence in your professionalism."

The girl's face puckered, and she struggled to keep her voice even as she asked, "Would you like me to get someone else to help you?"

"No," Gertrude said quickly. "We don't want to get back on *the list*. Calvin here might die of old age before the next salesgirl comes along."

Calvin gave Gertrude a dirty look but said only, "She needs a phone."

"OK then," the blue-haired girl said. "My name is Zandra and I would be happy to help you."

"*Zandra?*" Calvin asked, appalled.

Zandra ignored him. "Are you a current customer of AmeriCell?" she asked Gertrude.

"No," Gertrude said. "I've never had a cellular telephone before."

The girl smirked. "OK then. Would you like a smartphone or would you like to start with something more basic?"

"I want the smartest phone you have," Gertrude said.

"OK, then, that would be this one." She walked over to the newest iPhone, which sported a hefty price tag.

"Maybe not that smart," Gertrude said.

The girl looked up, her hand still doing a Vanna White toward the iPhone.

"How about your smartest phone that only costs a penny?"

The girl gave a disappointed nod and walked toward the Samsungs. "Here you go," she said.

"I'll take it," Gertrude said.

"Not so fast," Calvin spoke up. "What's the catch?"

"What do you mean?" Zandra asked.

"I mean, what are the terms of the contract?" he said condescendingly.

"What happened to your grampa voice?" Gertrude muttered.

"I'm trying to protect you," he muttered back.

Gertrude looked up at him in surprise. She felt a little flutter in her belly. She didn't think anyone had ever tried to protect her before.

"Well, it's a standard two-year contract," Zandra said. "If you'd like to have a seat, I can go over your options."

The chairs were absurdly tall. "These aren't chairs. They're bar stools," Calvin said.

Zandra ignored him and fiddled with her mouse. "So," she said, unfolding a pamphlet in front of them both, "here are your options. You choose how many minutes, how many texts, and how much data you'll need …"

Several minutes and a few signatures later, an annoyed Calvin and an excited Gertrude left the AmeriCell store with a shiny new toy. Zandra had offered to teach Gertrude how to use the Android, but Calvin had insisted he would teach her.

Back in the Cadillac, Calvin tried to keep his word, but he failed. "I don't understand," he said. "There's only one button."

"These are buttons," Gertrude said, trying to stab at an icon, but Calvin yanked the phone out of her reach.

"Don't go messing with it," he said. "I don't want to have to go back in there. Can't believe they employ blue-haired, tattooed, pierced hoodlums."

"Well, how are we going to use it if we don't know how to use it?"

Calvin sighed. "I have an idea."

Gertrude waited. Calvin started the car and pulled out of the parking lot.

"Well, are you going to share this idea with me?" Gertrude asked.

"We can go ask my granddaughter for help."

"Your stripper granddaughter?"

"Don't call her that," Calvin snapped. "And yes. But don't you dare mention that you know she is a stripper. We don't know that, do you understand me?" Calvin sounded downright menacing.

"Yes," Gertrude said.

"Is she in that folder? I don't know where she lives. Her name is Shelly Stevens, unless she's gotten married, which I doubt she has since she's taking off her clothes for strangers for a living."

Gertrude looked in the folder. "She lives at 7 Bean Street, and how could your granddaughter get married without you knowing?"

"I told you. I don't talk to my daughter much."

"You never told me that."

"Well, I'm telling you now. Where's Bean Street?"

"How should I know? Stop right here. I'll go in and ask for directions."

Calvin pulled the car over. "Here?"

"Yes, here."

"This is a funeral home," Calvin said.

"I can see that."

"Most people stop at gas stations for directions."

Gertrude looked around. "Do you see any gas stations?" She started to get out of the car.

"Stop," Calvin said. Then he rolled down his window. "Excuse me," he said to a woman with ridiculously red hair who was walking a basset hound. "Can you tell me where Bean Street is?"

She stopped walking. The basset hound looked relieved and lay down. "Sure," she said from across the street. "Go back to the light and turn left. Go about a half mile until you see Maple Street. Then bang a left. Then Bean will be the third or fourth street you cross."

"Thank you," Calvin said and rolled up his window. The woman said something inaudible and then dragged the reluctant basset back into action. Calvin pulled back into the street and said, "What is wrong with these people's hair?"

"You're just jealous because they have some."

Calvin didn't respond. He just drove to Bean Street with his jaw clenched. Gertrude was surprised that he was still involved in this escapade at all.

Seven Bean Street was a tiny lot occupied by a tiny, dilapidated house. Calvin groaned as he shut the engine off.

"Ready?" Gertrude asked.

"There is just no need of this," Calvin said.

"No need of what?"

"Of her living like this. Crows have always been hard workers. They've always lived respectably. This is disgusting."

Gertrude didn't know what to say, so she climbed out of the car, retrieved her walker from the back seat, and headed toward the door. After a small hesitation, Calvin was behind her. Gertrude knocked on the door, and a woman who looked too old and too chubby to be a stripper opened it.

Her eyes didn't even give Gertrude a look, but flew right to Calvin's face. "Dad?"

"Hi, Melissa."

Melissa could not have looked more shocked. She stepped back to allow them entrance. Gertrude led the way into a neat living room full of well-worn furniture and toddler toys.

"Please have a seat," Melissa said. "Can I get you anything to drink?"

"Do you have any Crystal Light?" Gertrude asked.

Melissa ripped her eyes away from her father long enough to give Gertrude a puzzled look. "No, sorry. But I have iced tea, hot tea, water?"

"Never mind then," Gertrude said and plunked down on the couch.

"No thank you," Calvin said and sat beside Gertrude, his feet straddling a plastic fire truck. "I take it Shelly has a little one?"

"Two actually, Conner and Drew."

"That's nice. Where are they?"

"Swimming lessons. They should be home soon. What are you doing here?"

"Well, this here is Gertrude. She's my neighbor. And she just got one of those new smartphones, and well, Shelly is the only young person I know. So I thought maybe she could help Gertrude figure out how to use it."

"It's kind of a stretch to say you *know* Shelly," Melissa said.

"Well, whose fault is that?" Calvin snapped.

They heard a car pull into the drive.

12

"Grampa?" Shelly asked, her surprise palpable. The two children who trailed her through the door stopped at her legs and looked up at Calvin.

He got up from the couch and took three steps toward her. Then he bent to give her an awkward, unreciprocated hug. "Hi, Shell," he said.

She dropped a bag on the floor, making an audible splat as wet towels hit the tiles. "What's wrong?" she asked.

Calvin forced a laugh. "Nothing!"

"Your grandpa here needs you to teach his girlfriend how to use her phone," Melissa said with ample snark.

"No, no," Calvin argued, and Gertrude was sure he was going to correct her nomenclature straightaway. Gertrude was mistaken. "Well, yes, I would like to have your help with the new phone, but that was really only a pretense for my visit."

Shelly's eyebrows went up. So did Melissa's. And Gertrude's.

"Oh?" Shelly asked, prodding him to continue.

"Well, I've just learned about the terrible death of a young woman across town, and well, it just got me thinking about you. She was about your age, I think, maybe a little older, but I just got ... well ... worried."

He didn't sound very convincing to Gertrude's ears, even using his granmpa voice, but Shelly seemed to buy it. "Well, I didn't even know her," she said. "I don't even think she was local."

"OK then, probably not. I know I didn't recognize the name. But, so, you're OK? Not hanging with any dangerous crowds?"

"What on earth are you up to, Dad?" Melissa asked, but Calvin didn't look away from Shelly's face.

"So, about this jitterbug?" Gertrude said, waving her phone in the air in an effort to break up some of the tension.

"Oh yeah," Shelly said, reaching out for the phone. "I'm sort of an expert. Used to work at C-mobile, but they didn't pay squat."

Calvin rolled his eyes, but Shelly didn't see that. She was looking at the phone.

"This is a nice one. OK, so, do you know how to turn it on and off?"

Gertrude shook her head.

Shelly showed her the power button.

"Maybe you should sit down," Gertrude said, and patted the couch beside her.

Shelly sat down. "So, if you have a tmail address, I can plug that in, and all your contacts should automatically transfer over."

Calvin snorted.

"What's tmail?" Gertrude asked.

Shelly looked at her mom.

Melissa shrugged.

"OK, well, tmail is the most popular email." She paused and looked at Gertrude doubtfully. "Email is electronic mail," she said, speaking painfully slowly. "Like, people can send you messages and letters and stuff."

"Oh! Nifty!" Gertrude exclaimed, sincerely delighted.

Shelly looked at her mom for guidance. Her mom didn't offer any. "So, what should your email address be?" Shelly asked.

"Gertrude?" Gertrude offered.

"That's probably already in use. Do you want to use your last name too, or maybe a middle name?" Shelly tried.

"Oh! I know!" Gertrude exclaimed. "Gertrude Gumshoe!"

Shelly paused, apparently speechless.

"Just do it," Calvin growled.

"OK, then. Your email address is," she spoke while typing, "gertrudegumshoe@tmail.com. Shocker.

Not taken. OK, so, you'll need a password. Make sure it's something you can remember."

"Cats," Gertrude said.

Shelly looked at her, confused.

"Cats is my password," Gertrude repeated.

"You should probably pick something more complex," Shelly tried.

"Just do it. No one is going to try to hack into this nut's email," Calvin said.

Gertrude gave him a dirty look.

"OK, then, you're good to go. Now you have an email address and a phone number. Do you know your phone number?" Shelly asked.

"A-huh. The girl with blue hair wrote it down for me."

"OK," Shelly said uneasily. "So if you want to send someone a text, you just tap this icon, and then type in their phone number. Then, write your message, and then hit this arrow, which means send."

"Wow!" Gertrude said. "Fancy."

"Now these things here," she showed Gertrude a screen full of icons, "are apps. There's an app for just about anything. Do you want me to set up any apps for you? Maybe Facebook or Twitter?"

Calvin snorted again.

"Twitter?" Gertrude repeated incredulously. "Is that an app that makes my phone tremble? How about a recorder? Is there an app that records conversations?"

"You mean phone conversations, or face-to-face ones?" Shelly asked.

"Both."

"Sure, let me look." Shelly found both apps, downloaded them, and showed Gertrude how to use them.

"Fancy," Gertrude said again.

"Anything else?" Shelly asked, sounding tired.

"Are there any cat apps?"

"Well, sure, there's one that sends you a cat picture every day."

"No, I mean an app *for* my cats."

"Of course not," Calvin said.

"Actually, there is. It's just a red dot that bounces around the screen, and there's some meowing going on in the background. It's actually quite annoying."

"Yeah, I want that one," Gertrude said.

"Of course you do," Calvin muttered. "If you turn that on in the car, I will kill you."

"Don't say that, Calvin," Gertrude said matter-of-factly. "If something happens to me, you'll be the first one they suspect."

"Oh, something's going to happen to you, all right," Calvin growled.

Shelly looked at her mom, her eyes begging for help.

"OK," Melissa said. "I think you got what you came for."

"Indeed," Gertrude said.

"So you didn't know the woman?" Calvin said.

"What woman?" Shelly asked.

"The dead one," Calvin answered.

"Nope. Don't think so," Shelly said.

"I hear she worked at that bar, Private Eyes," Calvin said. "You ever go in there?"

Melissa raised an eyebrow, but Shelly's face stayed straight, much to her credit, Gertrude thought. "I've been in there, yes, but I didn't see her."

"I hear she used to hang around with a girl goes by the name of Trixie," Calvin said.

Now Shelly looked suspicious. "Don't know her either."

"OK, then," Calvin said. "I'll get out of your hair. You just, um, be careful, OK?"

"OK," Shelly said uncertainly.

Calvin gave her another stiff hug, gave his daughter a curt nod, and then took a few steps to tousle the boys' hair.

And then they were outside and on their way to the car. Gertrude found it frustratingly difficult to stare at her phone and maneuver her walker simultaneously, so she slid the phone into her walker pouch.

13

"Now what?" Calvin asked, as he pulled the car out of the driveway.

"Maybe we should just go see the mayor. I could use my app to record his confession."

Calvin scoffed. "I should have known when you asked for that app. You won't get within a hundred yards of the mayor."

"Why not?"

"Because … well, because you're *you*."

"Fine. Then we need to find Trixie."

"Right, but how? I still don't think the bar is open. Plus, I'm not going in there," Calvin reminded her.

"Want to try her house again?" Gertrude asked.

"Not especially."

"We don't have to talk to her. Let's just go see if she's there. Then if she is, we'll just follow her, make sure she's OK?"

"And what if she's not OK? What are we going to do? Get out and thump the murderer with your walker?"

"No, you big meanieface, we're going to use my shiny new phone to call the cops."

"OK fine. We'll go see if she's home. But I'm not promising anything else after that."

"Deal," Gertrude agreed.

Trixie wasn't home.

"Now what?" Calvin asked again.

"I don't know," Gertrude said thoughtfully. "I wish we could just go talk to the cops. They may know things that would help us."

"Like what?"

"I don't know. Maybe they have DNA evidence or something? Phone records? They might know what kind of gun was used."

"You watch too much TV. They don't have any of that information yet. Those tests take time, and money. I doubt Somerset County is going to invest millions of dollars to figure out who killed a stripper. They're probably doing it the old-fashioned way, just like we are," Calvin said. Then he added, "Well, maybe not *this* old-fashioned."

Gertrude thought for a minute. Then she said, "They might've found the gun. It might be registered to someone."

"OK, so you're saying you want to go talk to the cops?"

"I think so. Don't you?" Gertrude looked at him.

"Not really."

"Why not?"

"'Cause I'm kind of embarrassed to be wrapped up in all this. I've got a better idea. Let's go talk to Frank—"

"Who's Frank?" Gertrude interrupted.

"And you think you're a detective? Maybe you should take notes. Frank Malone, the cop, the man from the second sex photo."

"I know who you meant. I was just testing you," Gertrude said.

Calvin sighed. "Well, let's go talk to him, not as a suspect, but as a cop. I've sort of got an in. Maybe he'll tell us what he knows."

Gertrude's eyes grew wide. "That's a great idea!" she said. "Great job, Watson!"

"I'm not Watson," Calvin grumbled. "If anything, *you're* Watson."

Calvin pulled into the Sheriff's Department lot and parked the car. Gertrude practically leapt out of her seat. She was so excited. She retrieved her walker from the back seat and headed toward the door before Calvin had even climbed out of the car.

"Can you wait a second?" Calvin called out.

"Hurry up, old man! Time's a wastin'!"

Gertrude did make it inside first, but then she stopped dead in front of the vast counter in the sheriff's department's lobby. She didn't know where to start.

Calvin walked right by her and approached the closest person in uniform.

"Can I help you, sir?" the deputy asked.

"Yes, I'd like to talk to Frank Malone. Is he in?"

"And can I ask what this is regarding?"

"I'm just an old friend. Wanted to talk with him for a bit. Won't take long."

The deputy looked suspicious, but he did look down at a computer screen. He pressed a few keys and then looked up at Calvin. "He's out on patrol right now. Do you want me to call him in?"

"Nah, can you just tell me where he's at? We can go to him."

The deputy glanced at Gertrude, who was still standing by the door. "You sure everything's all right?"

"Just peachy," Calvin said, and tried to smile.

"What's your name?" the deputy asked.

"Calvin. Calvin Crow."

"OK, then, let me give him a call." The deputy picked up a radio mic and said, "Somerset 15, Somerset 15?"

"Somerset 15, go ahead," a voice replied.

"Got a Mr. Calvin Crow here says he wants to talk to you. Are you close, or do you want him to come to you? He says he's willing."

"Sure, I can meet him at Gifford's ice cream scoop. Be there in ten," Frank said.

"OK, I'll let him know."

The deputy turned back to Calvin.

"Gifford's. Got it. Thanks a lot."

Calvin headed toward the door.

Gertrude followed him out. "Oh, goodie," she said. "I do love a good cotton candy cone."

Gertrude ordered a triple scoop of cotton candy ice cream with butterscotch topping.

"I thought you were broke," Calvin said, disgusted.

"I am, but I've got a Gifford's gift card."

Calvin rolled his eyes.

The kind-eyed woman in the green apron handed the blue ice cream through the small window.

"Thank you," Gertrude said, taking it with one hand. With the other, she began taking napkins from the nearby dispenser, which would only allow her to remove one napkin at a time. The people behind her in line waited patiently as she plucked each napkin.

After she'd taken ten, Calvin finally said, "Enough! You don't need any more napkins!"

Gertrude glared at him. "You won't be saying that when we've got a crisis and I've got the napkins!"

Calvin started toward an empty picnic table. "Oh sure," he said without turning to look at her, "my life is just full of crises that can be solved with a napkin."

"Crisises!" Gertrude hollered after him, causing everyone within a hundred feet to look at her to see what was wrong. She was still standing directly in front of the window.

Calvin turned too. "What?"

"Crisises! Not cris-*eeze*."

Calvin ignored her and sat down.

"Will you get back here?" Gertrude hollered.

"Why?"

"Because I can't carry an ice cream cone and use my walker at the same time."

"Maybe you should have thought of that before you ordered a triple scoop with sticky topping!" Calvin hollered.

The kind-eyed woman, who was now trying to help the helpless person behind Gertrude, wasn't kind-eyed anymore. Gertrude was indignant. "Will you get over here?" she yelled. "You're causing a scene!"

Calvin grunted and got up, stomped over to Gertrude and started to take her walker away.

"Don't touch my walker!" Gertrude said, appalled.

"Well, what do you want me to do?" said Calvin, exasperated.

"Take the cone," Gertrude said slowly, as if speaking to a stupid child.

"I don't want to touch your cone," Calvin said.

"Why not?"

"Ma'am, if you could just step aside," the kind-eyed woman tried.

"Because it's dripping butterscotch goo everywhere!" Calvin cried.

"Ahah! A napkin crisis already!" Gertrude declared.

"Excuse me, miss, I'd be happy to carry your cone," a deputy said, stepping alongside the odd couple. "Hi, Calvin," he said, nodding to Calvin as he took the cone from Gertrude's clutch. She handed him several napkins as well. "Where we headed?" he asked.

Wordlessly, Calvin headed toward the picnic table.

"Ladies first," the deputy said, motioning with his free hand toward the path Calvin had taken.

"Are you Frank?" Gertrude asked.

"I am," Frank said.

"Good," Gertrude said, and padded after Calvin.

When she had settled onto the bench, and Frank had returned her cone to her, and she had begun to hastily lick at the dripping butterscotch goo, Frank asked, "So, what's up, Calvin?"

"Well, we were just wondering—" Calvin began.

"We wanted to know where you were last night," Gertrude interrupted.

"Gertrude!" Calvin barked.

"Where I was?" Frank laughed. "Why?"

"So we can clear you of Lori Hicks's murder."

Frank's smile faded. "I'm sorry, who are you?" Frank asked.

"Gertrude," she replied and licked her ice cream cone.

"You'll have to excuse my friend," Calvin said. "She's a little, uh ... well, touched."

"Am not," Gertrude said, and took another lick.

"Of course, we know you had nothing to do with the crime. It's just that Lori was a friend of Gertrude's, and she's really worried, and we were wondering if you had any information you could share with us, you know, something that could ease Gertrude's uh ... her anxiety."

"I can't tell you anything," Frank said. "It's an open investigation."

"I understand," Calvin said, looking embarrassed.

"Have you found the murder weapon?" Gertrude asked.

Frank just stared at her.

"What would you say if I told you I knew where it was?" Gertrude asked and took another lick.

"I'd say you'd better tell me right now, or I'll arrest you for obstruction."

"Aha!" Gertrude said triumphantly. "So you haven't found it yet!"

Frank glared at Calvin. "Is there anything else you need? Because I need to get back to work."

Before Calvin could answer, Gertrude asked, "Did you know Lori Hicks?"

"No, I did not," Frank said.

Gertrude examined his face closely. "Huh," she said.

"What?" Frank asked.

"I'm not so sure you're telling the truth," Gertrude said thoughtfully.

"Of course I'm telling the truth! OK, I'm going now. You two don't call me again unless you actually need something, something that I am bound by my job description to provide." He spared Gertrude another disgusted glance and then stalked off toward his cruiser.

"Loser," Gertrude muttered.

"What is wrong with you?" Calvin asked, wide-eyed.

"I'm touched, remember?"

14

Trixie still wasn't home. Gertrude and Calvin sat there, in the car, staring up at her empty abode.

"Private Eyes has food," Gertrude said.

"I'm not going back in there. I told you that already. I'm not going to change my mind about that."

"OK then, just go drop me off. I'll just call you if I need anything."

"How are you going to call me?" Calvin asked.

"With my shiny Samsung."

"I know, but *I* don't have a cell phone, so what number do you plan to dial?"

"Oh shoot, we should go get some walkie talkies!" Gertrude exclaimed.

Calvin groaned. "I'm not spending any more money on this insanity."

"Of course not. Don't be ridiculous. I've got a whole collection of walkie talkies back at my place. Let's go!"

Calvin backed out into the street with a look on his face that fully amused Gertrude. He actually looked excited. But by the end of the five-minute drive back across town to Gertrude's trailer park, he had managed to hide whatever excitement still existed. He pulled into Gertrude's short driveway. She opened her door.

"You coming?" she asked.

Calvin looked at her trailer skeptically. "I'm not sure I should."

"Oh, don't be such a lily-liver. Come on."

Grudgingly, Calvin got out of his car, and with great trepidation, he ascended the few steps to Gertrude's door, which she had already flung open. He stepped inside and gasped.

His eyes scanned the trailer, growing wider and wider as they did so. After several seconds, his eyes rested on a neatly stacked collection of lampshades.

"Gertrude?" Calvin asked.

"Yeah?" Gertrude called, already out of sight amid the stacks.

"How many lampshades does one woman need?"

"You never know!" Gertrude called out. "Someone might have a lampshade crisis!"

As Calvin stared disbelievingly at the lampshade tower, a cat weaved through his legs, and Calvin let out a high-pitched wail.

Gertrude came hurrying back, a box balanced atop her walker. "What? What's wrong?"

"Nothing," Calvin said, panting, and leaning on a stack of encyclopedias, "just a cat."

"Oh, for Pete's sake," Gertrude said. "I thought the mayor had gotten you. Here, pick out one you like." She pushed her walker closer to Calvin, so he could peer in at the collection of walkie talkies.

"Gertrude, do any of these actually *work*?"

"Oh sure. I'm sure some of them do. We should probably test them before push comes to shove."

"Right." He reached in and grabbed one gingerly. Then he blew on it, and a cloud of dust flew off. He turned it on. "I'll be darned."

"What?"

"It appears to be working," Calvin said, astounded.

Gertrude pulled another one out of the box. It looked like something straight out of a World War II museum. She turned it on. "Channel 67," she said.

Calvin looked down. "I'm already there," he said.

"Hello?!" Gertrude hollered into her walkie.

"Good grief, Gertrude! I'm right here! You don't need to holler!"

"Did you hear me?" Gertrude asked.

"Yes, everyone in the county heard you!"

"No, I mean, did you hear me the through the walkie talkie?"

"How should I know? I'm deaf now!"

Gertrude stared at him blankly.

Calvin took a deep breath. "OK, let's try again. Take six steps *away* from me, and then *whisper* into the radio."

Gertrude nodded. She turned to walk away, wondering why he was taking this whole sound check thing quite so seriously. She stepped around a corner in her path so she was out of sight. "Are you ready?" she called out.

"Yes!" Calvin said, sounding utterly exasperated.

"Hello?" she whispered into the walkie. "Are you there?"

Calvin laughed. "Man, if anyone else is manning this channel, they just got the fright of their lives."

"Why?" Gertrude asked, coming back around the corner.

"Because you just sounded like an irate Miss Trunchbull."

"Who's Miss Trunchbull?"

"Never mind," Calvin said.

"So, it worked?"

"Yes, it worked," Calvin said.

"Great, let me just grab some extra batteries." She disappeared into the stacks again, and returned seconds later with a plastic grocery bag full of batteries.

"I doubt we'll need that many, Gertrude," Calvin said.

"You never know," Gertrude said, heading for the door.

"Right, 'cause there might be a battery crisis," Calvin said, and followed her.

Calvin drove Gertrude back to Private Eyes and then parked in the back.

"What are you going to do while I'm gone?" she asked him.

"Sleep."

"Well, then how am I going to call you for help if you're asleep?"

Calvin reclined his seat with a thump. "I'm a light sleeper."

"Calvin! I'm relying on you for my safety!"

He laughed as he settled in and closed his eyes. "Well, then you'd better not get yourself into any danger." He put his arm over his eyes.

Gertrude just sat there staring at him.

"Just go," he said, without moving his arm to see her. "I predict you get bored and come back within twenty minutes."

"Fine," Gertrude said. She flung the door open and hefted herself out of the car. *I'm going to show him. I won't get bored. I won't come back to the car. I'm going to stay in this strip club all night if it kills me.*

Gertrude was back in twenty minutes.

"Told you so," Calvin muttered.

"I'm not back," she said. "I just need some cash. I had enough to get in, but it turns out they won't let me just sit there without drinking something."

"Oh great," Calvin said, "so when you do come back, you'll be all sauced? I'm not sure I can handle a drunken Gertrude. I can barely stand you sober."

"Oh, just give me the money already. I'm just going to drink ginger ale."

He handed her a twenty. "I expect you to pay me back for this."

"Of course," she said, taking the twenty. "Every penny." She shut the door, wondering if there was a reward for catching Lori's killer. There should be, she decided.

Gertrude went back into the bar, settled back into the chair she'd left, and ordered a ginger ale from the wary waitress.

"That'll be two dollars," the woman in the pink bikini said.

"Two dollars? For a soda? Are you bonkers?"

The woman put her hand on her hip and sighed. "Do you want the drink, or not?"

"Don't you get cold?" Gertrude asked.

"How 'bout I go get the manager?" she said.

"OK, OK, here's a twenty. How 'bout you run me a tab?" (She'd always wanted to say that.) "Just let me know when I'm getting close to twenty dollars, and then cut me off." She laughed. The woman didn't. She snatched the twenty out of Gertrude's hand and turned to go. *Some people just have no sense of humor.*

126

Gertrude turned her attention to the small stage, but nothing was happening there yet. She looked around the dimly lit establishment for Trixie, but didn't see her. She got up and headed for the back, where she knew the dressing room was.

She made it all the way to the back wall when a man approached her. "Can I help you?" he said pleasantly enough.

"Yes, I'm looking for Trixie."

"OK," he said, "well, she'll be dancing a little later."

"So she's OK?" Gertrude asked.

"Yes, why wouldn't she be?" he asked.

"I mean, you've actually seen her?"

The man stared at her. "Yes. I've seen her," he said very slowly.

"OK then. I'll just go back to my table and wait for her turn at the pole." Gertrude gave him a fake smile and turned back toward her table.

Gertrude had drank four glasses of ginger ale and made three trips to the bathroom when she realized she was undeniably, miserably bored. Much unlike her expectations, the strip club was an incredibly dull place to hang out. The dancers were certainly talented young ladies, but their routines were spectacularly redundant, and Gertrude had quickly grown tired of watching the front row of men watch these redundant routines, enraptured. Trixie had been out to dance, twice, and then had disappeared into the back again. By the time the server approached her to offer her another refill, Gertrude had learned her name was Candy.

"Candy, this jitterbug has games on it, right?"

Candy looked at the phone in Gertrude's hand.

"Yeah," she said.

"Can you show me how to find one? I'm incredibly bored."

Candy set her small tray down on Gertrude's table. "Why are you here?"

"I like ginger ale."

"No, really," Candy repeated. "I mean, you don't have to tell me, but it just seems pretty weird."

"I'm waiting for Trixie," Gertrude said.

"Trixie's here."

"I know."

"Well, do you want me to go get her for you?" Candy offered.

"No, thank you."

Candy eyed Gertrude carefully. "Well, then why are you waiting for her?"

"I'm just here for her protection."

Candy stared at Gertrude for an elongated moment and then just turned and walked away.

Finally, the interminable evening appeared to be coming to an end. Trixie was at the pole when the bartender rang a bell and hollered, "Last call." Gertrude had long since polished off her tenth and final ginger ale. Two songs later, Trixie gave a final twirl and then stepped off the stage and headed toward the back. Two men started escorting people toward the door. Gertrude headed toward the back. One of the men took her by the arm. "Time to go," he said.

"I'm going," Gertrude said. "I'm just going to go with Trixie."

"No, you're not."

Gertrude kept going in her own direction, and the man physically prevented her from doing so. "Get your hands off me!" Gertrude cried. She was so frustrated she wanted to scream. Who did this guy think he was?

Another man appeared on the other side of her and took her by the other arm. She did scream. She screamed at the top of her lungs, and she started to wiggle her whole body with all her might. This only caused them to tighten their grips. They began pulling her toward the door, the second man dragging the walker along behind him. And in this way, they actually pushed Gertrude out of the closed club and into the nighttime dark. As they slammed and locked the door behind her, she stopped screaming.

She had absolutely no idea where Trixie was.

She groaned and began to walk around the building to the back, where Calvin was parked. She was about halfway down the narrow alley that led to the small parking lot in the back when a door to her left opened, scaring the wits right out of her. She would've screamed, but she was all screamed out.

15

"What are you doing here?" Trixie snapped.

"Nothing," Gertrude said.

"Really? 'Cause everyone is telling me that I've got some weird old lady stalking me."

Gertrude gasped. "I'm not old!"

"Look, lady, can you just leave me alone?"

"I'm trying to protect you!" Gertrude cried.

"Protect me? From what?"

"From the mayor!"

Trixie closed her mouth and stared at Gertrude for several long seconds. Then she stepped back inside and closed the door behind her. And Gertrude continued to Calvin's car.

When she climbed in, he said, "Well?"

"Well nothing. Trixie is an ungrateful brat, and I have to pee."

"Didn't they have a restroom in there?"

"Yes, but the bouncers threw me out."

Calvin looked at her, his eyebrows raised. "Seriously?"

"Yep. Literally. Threw. Me. Out."

"Huh. Well then. I'm actually impressed. So, now what?"

"Now we wait for Trixie to come out, and then we follow her."

Calvin groaned. "I don't think that's such a good idea."

"It's the only way, Calvin. And you know it."

"Fine. You think she'll come out the front or the back?"

"No idea," Gertrude admitted.

"Well, should we split up? You watch the front and I'll watch the back?" Calvin suggested.

"Why do I have to watch the front?"

"Because this is your idea!" Calvin cried.

"Fine," Gertrude said. "Call me on the walkie if you see her." Gertrude climbed back out of car and slammed the door. She retrieved her walker from the back seat and then slammed that door too. Then she made her way back down the dark alley and around to the front. She crossed the street, which was quiet this late at night, and crouched behind a mailbox on the opposite sidewalk. It wasn't an ideal hiding place, but she was in a shadow cast by the streetlight, and she hoped Trixie wasn't very observant.

Sure enough, Trixie came out the front door, looked both ways, and then, deciding she wasn't being watched, headed down the street.

"Calvin!" Gertrude whispered into the radio.

"Yeah?"

"She just came out. She's on foot. Come pick me up, but be stealthy about it."

Calvin didn't respond, but Gertrude could still sense his disgust. Still, within thirty seconds, Calvin eased his Cadillac out of the dark alley, and Gertrude stepped out of her hiding place. His headlights still off, he pulled the car alongside the curb. She hurried around the front of the car and, after hastily shoving her walker into the back seat, she climbed in.

"OK," Gertrude whispered, pointing down the street. "She went that way."

"I don't think you have to whisper."

"OK, follow her," Gertrude said. "But go slow."

"Yes, ma'am," Calvin said, obviously irritated by being bossed around.

"Don't call me ma'am," Gertrude said, oblivious of his irritation.

"Is that her?" he asked.

Gertrude gasped. "Yes! That's her! Slow down!"

"I can't go any slower Gertrude, or I won't be moving at all."

"Well, then stop the car."

Calvin pulled over to the side of the street. "Sure, this isn't suspicious at all."

"Oh stop it. There's no one around. Besides, we're not breaking any laws."

Calvin tapped the steering wheel with his fingertips, waiting all of thirty seconds before asking, "OK, can we go now?"

"Just hold your britches."

Calvin sighed.

Gertrude waited until Trixie was just out of sight and then said, "OK, easy now."

Calvin pulled the car back out into the street and drove in the direction Trixie had walked. They caught sight of her just in time to see her turn right down a side street. Calvin groaned.

"Where on earth is she going?" Gertrude wondered aloud.

"I think I know, and I don't want any part of it."

"What? Where is she going?"

"This is Frank's street."

"Frank the cop?"

"Yep."

"The house where Frank the cop lives with his wife?" Gertrude asked.

"Yep."

"OK, well, let's go down it. It's not a dead end, is it?"

He pulled the car over. "No, it's not, but Gertrude, I just don't want to do this anymore. If she's going to a cop's house, she's obviously going to be safe."

"Unless the cop's the murderer."

"I thought you said the mayor was the murderer."

"Well, we don't really know that yet, do we?"

"OK, well, I know that Frank is no murderer, so I'm going home. If you want to get out, do it here."

"Seriously? You're going to abandon me in the middle of town in the middle of the night?"

"Well, I'd rather not. I'd rather you just go home like a normal person, and I would be happy to give you a ride. But if you're going to insist on following this stripper around, yes, I'm going to leave you here."

"Fine," Gertrude said in a huff. She climbed out of the car and slammed the door. Then she opened the back door, made a big show of wrestling her walker out of the back, and then slammed that door too. And then, without so much as a glance, she walked away from Calvin and his car. Then she had a realization. She turned around and headed back toward the car.

He rolled down the window. "Not sure of the address," he said, "but it's before the street turns, big green house on the right."

"Thank you," she said, and then tried to hold her chin high as she stomped off indignantly. She heard Calvin pull the car away from the curb, and was overcome with the sudden realization that she was alone. All alone. In the dark. On a strange street. With nothing but a walker, a walkie talkie, and a jitterbug she wasn't quite sure how to make a call with. *Well, if I get into trouble, I'll just call Calvin with the walkie talkie. He might come back if I was in danger.* Gertrude took a deep breath and headed down the street.

It took her a while to reach the green house, and she was huffing and puffing by the end of her walk. When she finally reached her destination, there was a cop car parked in the drive. *So this is the right place. And he's probably home.* But Trixie was nowhere in sight. Gertrude spotted a nearby bush that was just about her size, so she walked over to it, with every intention of crouching behind it. Then she decided that was far too much work, so she plopped right down on her fundament. *There. That's better!* She relaxed for a second and then she peered around the bush at the house.

And she saw absolutely nothing of interest. It was a house, for sure, a green one. Its porch light was on, and it cast a weak light over the porch and most of the front yard. She stared at it, trying to see something, anything of interest. But there was nothing. *Fine. I'll just sit here,* she decided. *If someone is getting murdered, I'll be sure to hear it.* She began to relax, and then she saw a light come on in the upstairs room. A second later, two figures appeared. One was definitely a female. She decided that was Trixie. And one was probably a male. The cop? It must be. She couldn't stand not knowing. She decided to creep closer. The front porch's light did not reach the side of the house where this upstairs window was located, so she was able to walk to the house under the cover of utter darkness.

When she reached the house, she realized there was latticework covering most of the wall, and that latticework was covered with the red leaves of autumn vines. *What a stroke of luck,* she thought. She surveyed the wall. Then she slipped her shiny new phone into her pocket, just in case there was anything through the window worth photographing.

She took a deep breath and reached up with her left hand to slip her short fingers through holes in the latticework. Once she had a good grip, she slipped off her left loafer and poked around the bottom of the latticework with her foot, until she found a foothold. Then, she very gingerly pulled up with her left hand and pushed up with her left foot until her weight was supported completely by the wall and her body was fully suspended a full six inches off the ground. *Well, I'll be darned-tootin'—it held!* She took another deep breath and then, pushing up with her left foot, she reached as high as she could with her right arm and quickly stove her stubby fingers into the vine, trying like mad to hang on to the spot where her hand had landed. She was able to. Then, scared to death of falling, she swung her right foot around in an absolute panic, trying to find purchase. Finally, she did, and then she clung to the latticework with all four limbs, trying to catch her breath. After about two minutes of rest, she gathered the courage and strength necessary to reach upward again with her left hand—and in this way, Gertrude managed to slowly climb up the wall toward the second-story window. After about fifteen minutes of climbing, Gertrude was about three feet off the ground when her right foot slipped. She cried out, sounding a lot like a wounded duck, and flailed her foot around trying to find another place to stick it, but it was no use. Slowly, both her hands began to slip from their grip, and then she was falling. She screamed like an exceptionally loud rabbit caught in a trap and then *thud*, Gertrude landed in the grass, her limbs all akimbo, her breath knocked completely out of her.

In seconds she heard footsteps approaching and absurdly thought it was Calvin coming to rescue her. But then she realized she was staring up at the barrel of a gun.

16

"What on earth is wrong with you?" Trixie asked, glaring down at her.

Gertrude tried to roll over, but she looked much like a chubby beetle stuck on its back. "Aren't you cold?" Gertrude asked. Trixie was only wearing underwear. Gertrude reached into her pocket and tried to be sneaky as she stabbed at the smartphone's screen, but Trixie took one quick step and then kicked the phone out of Gertrude's hand. "Ow!" Gertrude accused.

"You really think you're going to call for help?" Trixie snapped. "No one is coming for you. You're going to die, just because you were stubborn and stupid. Now, get up, and get inside."

Gertrude tried to roll over again, but failed. "Where's Frank?" she asked.

Trixie laughed. "Frank's not going to rescue you either. You didn't think I heard you when you started to climb the vines? You sounded like a herd of elephants. I told Frank it was just a fat cat, but I had a feeling it was you, so I tied Frank to the bed."

"What, you going to kill him too?" Gertrude asked.

"Of course not!" Trixie cried. "I'm not going to kill him. I *love* him! I did all this *for* him! I just had to tie him up so I could deal with *you*, you crazy wench. Now, get up! I'm not going to tell you again!"

"I can't! Can't you see I'm disabled? You're going to have to help me."

"I'm not touching you. Now *get up*," she said through gritted teeth. Gertrude could tell she was getting worried. *Poor little Trixie doesn't know what to do.*

"Why'd you kill Lori?"

"None of your business."

"I'll get up if you tell me."

"You'll get up now, or I'll shoot you in the head."

"No you won't. Calvin is parked at the end of the street. He knows I'm here. He'll call the cops."

Trixie looked at the end of the street. Then she looked down at Gertrude. "Get up. Then I'll tell you whatever you want to know."

It hurt, but Gertrude managed to get herself rolled onto her side. Then, painstakingly, she rolled onto her belly. Then she did half a push up, cried out in anguish, and collapsed on the ground.

"Oh, you stupid freak!" Trixie reached down and tried to grab Gertrude's arm, and Gertrude swung one chubby leg at Trixie's feet. This knocked Trixie off balance and she let go of Gertrude's arm to catch herself with her free hand. Then, with all her gumption, Gertrude used the same leg to kick at the gun, which went off in Trixie's hand, momentarily freezing Gertrude with fear. But she soon realized she wasn't in any more pain than usual, so she figured she hadn't been shot, and began to scramble on all fours toward Trixie, fully intent on scratching her eyes out.

"Oh my … you crazy old hag, you are really nuts," Trixie said, and punched Gertrude in the face.

Gertrude's head snapped back from the blow, and she put her left hand to her cheek in surprise. "Ow! That hurt!" Gertrude reared up on her knees and tried to hit her back with her right hand, but missed Trixie entirely and flopped back down on her chest.

"Will you just stop!" Trixie cried, out of breath.

Gertrude did stop. She was just too tired to continue. She rolled over onto her back and looked up at Trixie. "Oh, just tell me why. I'm going to die anyway. Can't you throw me a bone?"

"Because I *love* him, and she wouldn't stop blackmailing him! I didn't mean to fall in love with him. I just did. And she didn't care! He told me to!"

"A cop told you to murder a waitress?" Gertrude asked, appalled.

"No, you idiot. Frank told me I had to get her to stop blackmailing him. Then he would leave his wife for me."

Gertrude started to laugh then. A great, deep belly laugh burbled up from deep within her and burst onto the scene, echoing through the neighborhood.

"Shut up!" Trixie hissed. "Will you just shut up!"

"You are bonkers! He wasn't gonna leave his wife! You killed her for nothing!"

"I didn't kill her—her greed did! I tried to warn her, to scare her off. Left her death threats at work, but she wouldn't stop. So I told her I was meeting Silas again at the water park. Said she could come for more pictures. Then we could threaten his business as well as his marriage—"

"Did you find the hide-a-key too?" Gertrude interrupted, picking her head up.

Trixie blinked, surprised. "No, I climbed through a window."

"Oh, should've just used a key," Gertrude said, lying her head back down. "Would've been easier."

The women heard sirens. Trixie looked up. Then she took off running. Into a neighbor's back yard. In her underpants. With the gun. Gertrude knew that it wasn't the cops. Gertrude knew that it was only an ambulance. But apparently Trixie didn't know her sirens. Gertrude lay there, trying to catch her breath as the sirens got closer and louder.

Then the ambulance pulled into the driveway, and its headlights lit up her spot on the lawn, which was now quite trampled. She lifted one weary, floppy arm in the air, just so they could see her. They must have, as she soon heard their footsteps running across the ground.

"Are you the one who pressed a LifeRescue button?"

Gertrude turned her head to the side and saw some bright orange New Balance tennis shoes. They were the most beautiful shoes she'd ever seen. "Yes," she said, "but I'm OK. I think. I just fell while trying to scale the wall. But you should call the police. Because there's a cop upstairs. He's tied up. And there's a murderer. She went that way." Gertrude pointed toward the neighbor's back yard. "She's in her skivvies. And she has a gun."

The man with the beautiful sneakers spoke into his radio. "Charlie one-one, send police to scene. Armed suspect, female, running west from this address."

A voice crackled through the radio, but Gertrude couldn't quite make it out.

"OK, ready?" a female paramedic scooched at Gertrude's head, preparing to lift her.

"Wait!" Gertrude cried. "My jitterbug!"

"Your *what?*" the female paramedic asked.

"My cellular telephone! It's over there!" she said, pointing through the grass. "We have to get it! I taped her confession!"

"I'll get it," Mr. Orange Sneakers said.

"Oh, thank you," Gertrude said. "Thank you so much." And then she closed her eyes.

17

G picked Gertrude up at the hospital. It was too early in the morning for the CAP bus, and she didn't know who else to call. She didn't really want to call Calvin. He'd almost gotten her killed with his negligence.

"Gertrude," G said when he saw her, "what on earth am I going to do with you?"

"Nothing. Just get me home. My cats must be starving."

G walked slowly alongside her as she edged her way out of the hospital. She was so happy to note that he had parked right outside the door.

"You really are the best, G," she said as he helped her into his truck. "Your wife is a lucky woman."

"Thanks, Gert," he said, as he put her walker in the back. He climbed into the driver's side. "So, what happened?"

"Well, you see, these kids stole Tornado. So I went looking for their mom at the strip club, but, as you know, she was in the House of Balls. I thought the mayor did it, but I guess it was a stripper named Trixie. Darn it."

G laughed. "Don't worry. The mayor will get his due eventually."

"Yep. Sooner than you may think too."

"What does that mean?" G asked.

"You'll see," Gertrude said.

"So, have you talked to the cops yet?" G asked.

"Yep. They were waiting for me at the hospital. And do you think they could say a simple 'thank you'? No! Nothing! They listened to my story and then just left! I figured there'd be some reward money at least!"

G laughed again.

"But I am going to adopt the murderer's cat, so that's the bright side."

"Is that right?"

"Yeah, I told the cops, and I called animal control. She has a beautiful gray tabby. It's not the cat's fault his human's a monster."

G shook his head. "I suppose that's true."

They were quiet the rest of the way to the trailer park. When G pulled in, Gertrude said, "Actually, can you take me to trailer number nine?"

"Sure, who's there?"

"My cat."

G helped her out of the truck.

She thanked him again.

"You sure you're all right here?"

"Absolutely," she said, already climbing the steps to the door.

"OK then," G said, and got in his truck to drive away.

Carl opened the door before Gertrude could even knock. "Hey, Gertrude! Did you hear? The cops caught the murderer!"

Gertrude rolled her eyes as she stepped into the trailer. "The cops didn't do squat. *I* caught the murderer."

"Oh," Carl said, and ran toward the living room.

"Good to see you," Joel said. "What's up?"

"Oh, I just figured you were going to take the kids back to Toledo, so I wanted to say goodbye to them." *And I was hoping you might give me some reward money for catching your ex-wife's murderer.*

"Oh, well, how nice. Yes, we're leaving today. The police finally told us that we could."

Carl came back in, holding Tornado squished up against his neck. "I suppose you want Tornado back," he said, pouting.

"Well, I do, but if you want him, you can have him. But you have to promise to take very, very good care of him. He's a—"

"Really?! Can we, Daddy, can we?" Carl asked, looking up at his father with pleading eyes.

Joel looked down at his son. "I don't think so, honey. I don't want to take a cat all the way to Toledo."

Carl burst into tears.

"Oh, I have an extra cat carrier," Gertrude said.

Joel gave her an exasperated look.

"Puh-lease, Daddy?" Carl begged.

Joel sighed. "OK, fine."

"Hooray!" Carl cried.

"I'll help you take care of him," Sophia said from behind Carl.

"Could I just have a minute with him?" Gertrude asked, holding out her hands.

"Sure," Carl said, and handed her the cat.

She pulled Tornado into her chest and then pivoted inside her walker space until her back was to the family. Then she pushed her face into Tornado's neck and shoulder. "I love you so much," she mumbled into his fur. "I'm going to miss you so, so much. But I think this little boy needs you more than I do, so you be good to him. But you remember me, OK? You always remember that Mommy loves you." She inhaled one more deep breath of him and then wiped her tears in his fur. Then she pivoted back around to face Carl and handed Tornado back to his ready arms.

"Thanks," Carl said softly.

"You're welcome," Gertrude said. "I'll go get that cat carrier now."

Three days later, Gertrude pounded on Calvin's door at ten minutes till nine.

He answered it immediately. "Did you find another dead stripper?" he asked.

"No, not yet," Gertrude admitted. "Why haven't you come to visit me?"

"Didn't want to."

"So, you just drop me off in the middle of nowhere in the middle of the night, and then you drive off, and I almost get killed, and you don't even come to say you're sorry?"

"Oh, for Pete's sake," Calvin said. "It wasn't the middle of nowhere, and *you chose* to get out of the car. I have nothing to apologize *for*. If anything, I would think that you should have come to me by now to say *thank you*."

"Thank you? Are you bonkers? What do I have to say thank you for?"

"Oh, never mind," Calvin said. "So, the news said she discharged a firearm. Did she try to shoot you?"

"Yep!" Gertrude said proudly. "Almost got me too. Would've if I hadn't a ducked!"

Calvin rolled his eyes. "So, did she say anything interesting to you?"

"Oh yeah! I got a full confession out of her! Recorded it on my jitterbug. They didn't put that on the news?"

"No, Gertrude, they sure didn't. So, why'd she do it?"

"Can I come in?" Gertrude asked. She was getting tired of standing.

"No, thank you. So, why'd she off her partner?"

"Well, she fell in love with Frank the cop. So she wanted to stop blackmailing him, but Lori wouldn't."

"Oh," Calvin said, thoughtfully. "So when Trixie said they were only blackmailing two men, she meant Silas and the mayor, huh? Tried to keep her boyfriend out of the equation?"

"Yep, I think so."

"So do you think she was going to take over the blackmailing?"

"I dunno. Probably not if she framed Silas," Gertrude said.

"So then why'd she break into your place to steal the photos?"

"Not sure," Gertrude admitted. "She never confessed to that part, although I didn't think to ask. I'm sure it was her. I think she probably just wanted to get the picture of her and Frank back. We could go visit her in jail if you want, and ask her?"

"No!" Calvin declared, alarmed. "I'm all done traipsing around with you. You have a nice day," he said, and started to close the door in her face.

"Wait!" she said, holding up one hand. "I came over to invite you to my press conference."

Calvin guffawed. "Press conference? What for?"

"I called one. I have news. So I called a press conference."

"Really?" Calvin said, his voice adrip with criticism. "Is there any press coming?"

"Oh, never mind then," she said, and turned to go. Then she had another thought. She reached into her walker pouch and then turned back toward Calvin. "Here, this is for your fridge," she said, with her hand outstretched.

He took her offering. "Well, I'll be darned," he said, looking down at her shiny new business card. "Not bad, Gert. Not bad."

"Don't call me Gert," she said, easing herself down his steps. "Only my friends call me that."

At nine o'clock sharp, a car pulled into Gertrude's short driveway. *What, no news van?*

A pretty, but frazzled-looking, reporter climbed out of the car. She headed toward Gertrude's door. Gertrude stepped outside to meet her. "Hello!" she said brightly, as she came down the steps. "Are you a reporter?"

"Yes," the woman said. "I'm Lindsey Michaels with Channel 5. Are you Gertrude?"

"Sure am!"

"OK, then, what do you have?" Lindsey asked, taking out a small notepad.

"Shouldn't we wait for everyone else?" Gertrude said.

Lindsey snickered. "I think you're lucky to get me, lady. So spill it."

Gertrude looked at the road, unsure of how to proceed.

"Either start talking, or the only reporter here is leaving," Lindsey said.

"But you don't even have a camera!" Gertrude complained.

Lindsey took a phone out of her pocket and wagged it at Gertrude.

"OK then," Gertrude said. She backed up a few feet and then stepped up onto the steps leading to her front door. In this way, she felt a little as if she were on stage. She had always dreamed of holding her own press conference. So what if there was only one press person present? She would just make the best of it. She cleared her throat. "I have called you here today"— Lindsey Michaels rolled her eyes—"to announce that I have decided to open my own private investigating services —"

"They gave you a PI license?" Lindsey Michaels interrupted.

Gertrude paused. *They have official licenses for this?* "Well no, not yet, I'll be working on that. But for now, I have this business card ..." she held up one of her new business cards. Lindsey rolled her eyes again. Gertrude hobbled down the few steps and handed the pretty reporter a card.

"Is this all you called me here for?" Lindsey Michaels asked.

"No, there's more," Gertrude said and went back up the steps. "As you see on the card, my business is called Gertrude Gumshoe Inc. —"

"You're incorporated?" Lindsey asked, raising an eyebrow.

Unsure of what she meant with this question, Gertrude ignored it. "What people don't know is that it was Gertrude Gumshoe Inc. who apprehended the fierce and dangerous woman who murdered Lori Hicks. And now I am making my services available to the public. For a fee."

"OK, I'm leaving," Lindsey said.

"No wait, there's more. At first, I suspected that the Mattawooptock Mayor, Lance Pouliot was the murderer."

For the first time, Lindsey Michaels looked interested. Or at least amused.

"But I was wrong. However, in the course of my investigation, I did find this incriminating photo of the Mattawooptock Mayor bedding the stripper-murderer." Gertrude pulled the photograph out of her back waistband.

Now, Lindsey took her phone out. Suddenly, Lindsey was the most engaged journalist in the state. Within three seconds, Miss Michaels had taken three photos of the photograph. "Any chance I can take that?" she asked.

"Promise to publish it?" Gertrude asked.

"Promise," Lindsey agreed.

"Here you go," Gertrude said, handing the pretty reporter the evidence of debauchery. "Thank you for coming to my press conference. Have a nice day." And with that, Gertrude Gumshoe went back into her trailer, and sat down in her recliner. She invited the cats to join her, which many of them did. Then she started a new episode of *Murder, She Wrote*, checked to make sure her shiny new cell phone was fully charged, and had a signal, and then sat back, relaxed, and waited for the calls to pour in.

CPSIA information can be obtained
at www.ICGtesting.com
Printed in the USA
LVOW01s1604240317
528386LV00007B/423/P